THE
LAST
GRAIL
KEEPER

THE
LAST
GRAIL
KEEPER

PAMELA
SMITH HILL

HOLIDAY HOUSE / New York

Sir Gawain and the Green Knight: A New Verse Translation by Marie Boroff.
Copyright © 1967 by W. W. Norton & Company, Inc. Used by permission.

The Mists of Avalon by Marion Zimmer Bradley. Copyright © 1983. Used by
permission of Scovil Chichak Galen Literary Agency, Inc.

Library of Congress Cataloging-in-Publication Data
Hill, Pamela Smith.
The last Grail keeper / by Pamela Smith Hill.—1st ed.
p. cm.
Summary: After an archaeological dig at Glastonbury Tor in England
uncovers the Holy Grail, Felicity and her mother, a professor of Arthurian literature,
find that their destinies are linked across time with the Grail
and the legendary King Arthur.
ISBN 0–8234–1574–0 (hardcover)
[1. Grail—Fiction. 2. Arthur, King—Fiction. 3. Magic—Fiction. 4. Space
and time—Fiction. 5. Archaeology—Fiction. 6. Glastonbury Tor (England)—
Fiction. 7. England—Fiction.] I. Title.

PZ7.H557215 Las 2001
[Fic]—dc21
00–053855

For Holly
and Stephen

Acknowledgments

Many thanks to everyone in my critique groups, especially Carmen Bernier-Grand, Carolyn Conahan, and Margaret Donsbach for reading the entire manuscript; to Eloise Jarvis McGraw, who taught me so much about writing and the writing life; to Graham Salisbury, for his suggestions on point of view; and to my husband, Richard, for navigating all those treacherous roundabouts and narrow country lanes on our pilgrimage to Avalon.

THE
LAST
GRAIL
KEEPER

Chapter 1

Digging Up Fairy Tales

There is every reason to believe the Holy Grail existed,
not perhaps as is commonly believed, but as part of
an ancient ritual administered by wise or holy women.
—Dr. Vanessa Jones,
Exploring the Myth of the Grail Keeper

The first thing you should know is that before this happened, I didn't believe in ghosts or ESP or fairy tales. Only one member of a family should believe in that stuff, and since my mom has made a whole career out of it, well, that let me off the hook.

More or less.

Because for almost as long as I could remember, I'd had this odd trick of knowing how things would turn out *before* they happened. Not ESP exactly, and not all the time—but like the day we met Ian Frazer. I was sure it wouldn't rain, so I set tea out on the terrace. But I'm getting ahead of myself.

1

On the day this all began, I'd just read an e-mail from Erin back home in Missouri. She'd gotten her learner's permit and was already halfway through a driver's ed class. "We practiced parallel parking today," she wrote, "and I did it perfectly the very first time. I'll get my license in August!" Meanwhile, I was stranded in Glastonbury, England, where the highways were narrow and crooked, everybody drove on the wrong side of the road, and the roundabouts at every intersection freaked Mom out so bad that *she'd* stopped driving—and wouldn't let me go near a steering wheel.

I had a bad case of cabin fever.

Okay, so I admit that our particular "cabin" came straight out of a storybook—Maiden's Cottage had a thatched roof, casement windows, and its very own eccentric tabby named Merlin. But a storybook setting only takes you so far; something has to happen, right? And up until then, nothing had.

I could sit around studying my *Missouri Driver Guide* (which I already knew by heart) or wait for Mom to walk home from a day of research or hang out in Glastonbury, where all the shopkeepers pretended to believe in magic and sold Morgan le Fey crystals to bunches of pathetic tourists. That's because a lot of people (including my mom) believed Glastonbury used to be the island of Avalon—you know, that place King Arthur went after his son or nephew or *whatever* had pretty much bashed the life right out of him. But who cares?

There were times, I confess, when Glastonbury Tor looked pretty amazing—a big, hulking mass against the sky. When the afternoon light made it swim in this thick golden haze, you could almost believe in magic. Almost. But on that particular day, the Tor just looked like a hunchbacked hill on the horizon. Nothing to write home about.

I leaned against the railing on Maiden's Bridge, just across from our cottage, and stared down at my beat-up copy of the *Missouri Driver Guide*. "I'll get my license in August." I could just *hear* Erin's voice, in that chirpy little gloat of hers. I was already sixteen—without even a learner's permit to my name because Mom was such a control freak. "You're not ready yet, Felicity," she always said. "You're cerebral, like me."

I reread that all-too-familiar passage in the manual. "Stop even with the vehicle ahead of the parking space. . . ." So there I was, in our yellow Volvo, moving alongside the car ahead of my

3

space, stopping perfectly when our rear bumpers were side by side, turning the wheel first to the right, then to the left. Or was it left, then right? I glanced back down at the page but couldn't find my place. All the words seemed blurry somehow, like grimy smudges on the refrigerator.

Then the smudges shifted; the words spiraled across the page and whirled themselves into patterns of brilliant purple lights. Shining, sparkling, glittering. They took shape, coiling into serpents and dragons, dancing in circles that came together and broke apart, spinning from top to bottom, bottom to top.

The shapes were back.

I'd seen them twice, maybe three times before, in dreams—wild, weird dreams that woke me up in a cold sweat. But in broad daylight? I closed my eyes and tried to will them away. But that only made things worse. The shapes grew brighter, clearer. They swirled faster, completely out of control. And I was swirling right along with them.

"Excuse me, miss," someone said.

I turned around so fast that all I could see was a spinning purple fog.

"Are you all right?" the voice asked, and I felt a strong hand reach out to steady me.

I couldn't help hoping that the voice belonged to a tall, handsome stranger, the kind you read about in those paperbacks you get in Safeway and pass around to your friends. But when the fog in my head had lifted, I saw an old guy, about Mom's age, his shirttail hanging out, his boots caked with layers of dried mud. He was still holding on to my arm—tight—as if he expected me to throw myself over the railing on Maiden's Bridge.

So I pulled away. "I'm fine. Really."

He stared at me a moment, then glanced down at a scrap of paper. "I'm looking for Dr. Vanessa Jones, Maiden's Cottage," he said. His voice was low and rumbly with a Scottish or Irish accent (I can never tell the difference). "Am I at the right place?"

I nodded. "Dr. Jones is my mom. I'm Felicity."

"Delighted," he said, shaking hands. "Ian Frazer, University of Edinburgh. I understand your mother visited the dig today."

"She should be home soon."

"Could I wait then?" he asked.

Once you got past all that mud and dirt, Ian Frazer was way different from all the other academic types Mom usually hung out with. His face was tanned, his dark hair graying around the temples. I even liked his neatly trimmed beard.

"Sure," I decided. "Why don't you stay for tea?"

I took Dr. Frazer out to the terrace, where I'd already set the table. The sun slipped behind the clouds and a low rumble of thunder rattled the casement windows. That's when he said, "You took a chance setting all this outside today."

And I said, "I don't think it's going to rain."

That's all I said about it. If it *was* ESP or something strange, I didn't want to talk about it, not with him, not with Mom, not with anybody.

I went back into the kitchen to put the kettle on, and stared out the pass-through at Dr. Frazer. What a contrast to Dr. Gildas, who headed up the dig at Glastonbury Tor. I'd met him a week or so before at a dinner party with Mom. Bald, fat, and *really* old—like most of the men Mom knew. Since Dad had remarried, Mom seemed more determined than ever to spend every possible moment working alongside the most unattractive people on the planet.

Suddenly, the front door slammed open, and Mom dashed inside. Her red hair had slipped out of its braid and her glasses were pushed up on her forehead at a wild, crazy angle. I swear, she must have run all the way home.

"The most incredible thing happened today," she announced, shouting into the kitchen.

"Incredible!" She dropped her pack on the dining room table, slammed her glasses down on her nose, and sat down to catch her breath. But not for long. "They've found something big. Really big. Security all over the place."

Mom started pacing across the living room, arms waving, hair flying.

"Calm down, Mom." I motioned her into the kitchen. "There's a professor from—"

"Listen to me, Felicity!" Mom stopped pacing and looked right at me. "We're talking armed security—and they wouldn't let me in! That's how big it is!"

Now that *was* interesting. I left the cake unsliced and walked into the living room. Everybody who was anybody in medieval studies knew my mom. Why, the books and papers she'd written about King Arthur and the Holy Grail would fill a library! She'd never been turned away from a dig—for as long as I could remember. Was that why Dr. Frazer had come? To apologize? I glanced out at the terrace.

"Mom." I took her elbow and started to guide her toward the bathroom, well out of Dr. Frazer's range. "There's someone—"

She broke away and headed for the phone. "Not now. I've got to find out what's going on."

"But all this Avalon stuff isn't even real. You can't dig up fairy tales."

Well, I should have known something really bizarre was going to happen, because I shivered—a real shiver—that ran up my spine and back down again. I knew if I closed my eyes, those serpent and dragon shapes would be back.

Mom gestured toward Glastonbury Tor with the phone. "That's no fairy tale out there." Then her voice dropped to a whisper. "Gildas has even called in an archaeologist from Scotland. Ian Frazer. Maybe he can tell me what's going on."

"That's what I've been trying to tell you!" I shook my head. "He's here, Mom."

She froze.

"On the terrace." I motioned toward the French doors.

Just then, Dr. Frazer filled the doorway.

"I couldn't help but overhear," he apologized. "Let me introduce myself properly."

Mom smiled weakly and extended her hand. "Nice to meet you." Then she turned toward me and whispered, "Why didn't you tell me?"

As if Mom had really given me a chance. I walked back to the kitchen to get the tea and cake. "Armed guards—that's pretty extreme, isn't it?" I said. Dr. Frazer didn't say anything. So I asked, "What have you found up there anyway?"

An awkward silence hung in the air. Really awkward.

I plunked the tea tray down on the table. Finally Mom said, "You haven't answered Felicity's question, Dr. Frazer." She poured the tea while I cut the cake. "What have you found? Something Arthurian, perhaps?"

Dr. Frazer placed his spoon precisely on the rim of his saucer. "It's too soon to know anything conclusive."

I passed him a piece of cake. "Well, if you haven't found anything conclusive," I said, "then no problem. Mom should be able to observe your work tomorrow."

"I'm afraid not." He turned away and gazed at the Tor. "Unless Dr. Gildas chooses to lift his ban on all visitors."

I nearly dropped a plateful of cake. Mom was *right*!

Then my hands started to shake and that chill in my spine came back. I should have sat down then and there, but you never know what you *should* have done until it's all over.

"Why did you come here?" Mom demanded.

"I've always admired your work."

"Don't patronize me," Mom snapped. "What is it, Frazer? A manuscript? A few blond hairs locked away in a casket? Or is it the Grail? The Holy Grail of ancient Britain?"

And that's when it happened.

The whole world started to dissolve like a '50s monster movie. Mom. Dr. Frazer. The garden. Far away, half hidden in shadows, I saw this thing, a kettle or a bowl, etched with intricate designs— serpents and dragons shimmering in purple light. They began to move and breathe and *live*. I heard their voices, moaning low and soft like a whippoorwill at twilight.

"Catch her, quick!" But that was Mom's voice. Then everything went dark.

Chapter 2

Where the Fire Cast No Glow

Had Arthur been an historic figure, then, without a doubt,
he would have been a contemporary of the sixth century
monk and historian, Gildas of Glastonbury.
Gildas, however, is as silent as the grave upon the subject
of King Arthur. Had such a great king existed, would Gildas
not have been obliged to record his deeds?
—Archibald Gildas,
"King Arthur: Beguiling the Legend,"
Journal of Modern Mythological Exploration

The next thing I knew, I was lying curled up like a baby in a dark, narrow passageway that smelled like centuries of rot and must and damp. It was the kind of place where you'd expect to find black widows or blue-tailed lizards. Or bodies long dead.

"Mom!" I cried. Her name choked in my throat. It was like I didn't have a voice anymore, or couldn't remember how to make the sounds that form words. Again, I called for help. Again, the words died silent.

I peered into the darkness. Could I move? Slowly, I flexed my little finger, my wrist, my arm. They were stiff, even sore, but they moved. I stretched out my legs and slowly got to my feet. My head brushed against the top of the passageway; my outstretched arms touched its sides. As far as I could tell, there was nothing but darkness ahead and behind me.

Like when the tour guide at Branson turns out all the lights in Marvel Cave, and you stand there feeling all alone, a sudden rush of fear in your chest. And just when you're ready to reach for a friend's hand, Erin's hand, the guide turns on the lights. But I was alone and there weren't any lights. That's when I remembered something Dad said to me once, just as he was leaving that last time: "Never look back." So I inched ahead.

Minutes, maybe even hours, passed. Anyway, they *seemed* like hours to me. And miles and miles of cold, damp, rotten darkness that twisted and turned on itself. I ran my hands along the sides of the passageway to keep my balance—and a sense of direction. At least, I told myself, I hadn't run into any skeletons.

Then, suddenly, there was a pale glow up ahead. I turned one corner, then the next, and the next. The glow grew brighter, the air warmer. I heard the crackle and pop of a fire—a big fire. I edged around one final corner.

It was Dr. Gildas!

Or was it?

True, he was as fat and smooth-faced as I remembered. But this old man, sitting on a stool in front of a great, roaring fire, was different somehow. His eyes were smaller, sharper. His face harder. He wore long, dark robes like some kind of priest. Jewels gleamed on his fingers. He unrolled a manuscript and laughed. A mean, ugly laugh. Then he threw the manuscript into the fire. He turned suddenly and looked right at me.

No, right *through* me. As if I wasn't there! And my inner voice, the one that was always telling me about things that hadn't happened yet, whispered, *You're nothing but a shadow.*

But I didn't completely trust that voice. Would you? So I flattened myself against the wall; it was cold through my pajamas.

Pajamas? Was this a dream?

No, said that voice again.

I scrunched down deeper. The dark, dank cavern felt alien, even hostile. So did the man who looked like Dr. Gildas.

But then I noticed something else—something gleaming and square, sparkling purple and gold. Irresistible. I edged closer. My skin tingled.

I moved so close, I could feel the heat from the fire, smell the old man's sweat. Then he turned sharply and spoke toward the corner where the fire cast no glow, just beyond the box of sparkles.

A shape—dark, tall, just barely there—moved out of the shadows toward the old man. A glint of gold caught the fire's light. A wave of sicky-sweet perfume rolled through the corridor.

My whole body started to shake uncontrollably. And I was hot, sweaty, sick. This huge wave of nausea rumbled across my stomach and pushed up my throat. My knees buckled. Then darkness swallowed everything up.

I woke up to a dim light in a tiny, closed space. Damp, like before, but smaller, and smelling of earth. My stomach growled. How could I be sick one minute, then hungry the next? This time, I bumped my head on the top of the passageway— hard; it must have shrunk—or I must have grown.

My shoulders brushed against the wall—one side stone, the other earth.

Could this be the same place, but changed somehow? Had time passed? *Maybe even centuries,* my inner voice whispered.

There were scraping sounds ahead. Flickering light. Slowly, I edged forward.

"Blast this lantern!" a man shouted.

I froze.

This time it *was* Dr. Gildas. He was kneeling on all fours, fiddling with a Coleman lantern. He sat back on his knees and started sorting through his pockets. "Where's that charm when you need it?" he asked, turning toward me.

Before I could answer, he turned away, as if he hadn't seen me. Was Dr. Gildas just talking to himself? "Superstitious bunk," he muttered.

Dr. Gildas steadied the lantern and pried open a heavy, metal chest. Purple and amber sparkles floated through the opening. The hinges on the chest squeaked when he lifted the lid and thrust both hands inside. Flashes of swirling shapes and creatures danced right before my eyes.

"Wait, you old fool!" came a voice right behind me. "Do you want to burn us past all recognition?" A burnt wisp of paper fluttered to the floor. "Use the charm."

The air was suddenly sicky-sweet all over again. My stomach heaved. I turned to see the shape of someone walking out of the darkness. But I couldn't see the face—I was suddenly too sick—only the gleam of a ring with a dark red jewel shaped like a dragon.

Most impressive, Miss Felicity Jones.

But the voice I heard then, a woman's voice, didn't belong to anyone I'd ever known.

Chapter 3

Not Quite ... Human

In all haste, the queen [in truth, Arthur's own mother] was sent for, and she brought with her Morgan le Fay, her daughter, that was as fair a lady as any might be. . . .
—Sir Thomas Malory,
Le Morte D'Arthur

And then I found myself in bed, back in my room at Maiden's Cottage. So, it had been a dream after all. Anyway, that's what I thought at first.

Why must you people always be so conventional?

It was that voice again, the one from my dream. A woman's voice with some kind of accent. I lay still, huddled under the covers, waiting for her to speak again. Then, after what seemed like forever, I came to my senses.

Of course, the voice belonged to somebody walking along the footpath outside, and I'd just dreamed that voice into my dream. A soft breeze moved through the filmy white curtains. Summer night sounds drifted up from the brook and trees below. But there weren't any voices. I crossed to the window. Outside, soft patches of moonlight splashed across Maiden's Bridge and the footpath. Nobody was there.

But looking at Maiden's Bridge suddenly brought everything back to me. Mom and Dr. Frazer . . . that humiliating tea party. I'd fainted dead away like a mindless romantic heroine—probably straight into Dr. Frazer's arms. Because when I came to, he was carrying me upstairs, and Mom was trotting alongside with that wild, panicked "Oh My Precious Baby" look on her face. That's why I'd woken up in bed—and that's why I'd had those bizarre nightmares.

Can you perceive nothing?

The woman's voice again.

I peered out into the moonlit darkness. Just where Glastonbury Tor should have been, I saw those shapes again. Swirling, dancing, flying. Were they calling to me? I shook my head and took a deep breath. The shapes disappeared all right, but my eyes were still playing tricks on me.

Because in the moonlight, Glastonbury Tor suddenly looked like it was floating, lifted ever so slightly above the ground—or swimming in a dark and shimmering sea. Mom always said that centuries ago, Glastonbury might have been an island, and for the first time, I believed her.

King Arthur's Avalon, my inner voice whispered.

I tried hard to silence that voice inside my head. But it wouldn't stop. *Avalon—where the Grail was buried. Under the Tor.*

Then that unseen woman spoke again. *Perhaps you will do after all, Felicity Jones.*

I whirled away from the window and gasped. The bedroom wall had become some kind of mirror. Within its reflection, a swirl of amber and purple lights outlined the shape of a woman. I backed against the curtains, shut my eyes, and counted to ten. Just as I opened my eyes, a woman stepped out of the wall, into my bedroom.

"Greetings, Felicity Jones."

I stepped back and crashed into an antique lamp, which I caught just in the nick of time.

My visitor didn't notice. She straightened the hem of her long, flowing cloak and said, "Time travel is so difficult. One never arrives feeling quite one's self."

So was this a nightmare?

"I assure you it is not," she replied.

My mouth dropped open. That woman, whoever she was, had answered my thoughts like some kind of mind reader.

"Anything less would have disappointed you."

"I didn't expect anything," I said.

The woman frowned. "May I sit down?"

I shook my head. Would you have wanted a perfect stranger sitting in your bedroom in the dark of night?

But she ignored me and sank into the old green velvet wing chair by the fireplace as if it were her own. "I am always surprised at how this, the most unenlightened century of all time, has nevertheless managed to improve on comfort." She adjusted a needlework cushion to fit precisely into the small of her back. "It is the one thing you people do well."

"What do you mean, 'you people'?" I asked.

"I do not live in your millennium," the woman answered.

This couldn't be happening, I told myself. I couldn't be standing in my own room, having a conversation with an apparition from a thousand years ago, or whatever. Dad used to say that if we could put a name to our fears, they would go away. So you know what I had to ask.

"I am Morgan le Fey, Lady of the Lake and sister to King Arthur," she said without batting an eye. "Who else would I be?"

So Dad's advice hadn't worked—again.

In fact, now things were even worse. Because Morgan le Fey wasn't real. Everybody knew that. What was it Mom had said the other night at dinner? That in all the old stories, Morgan le Fey was a fairy . . . or a witch! She had never been quite . . .

"Human." Lady Morgan finished another one of my thoughts.

I edged toward the door and tried to smile politely. "I don't mean to offend you, Ms. le Fey, it's just that . . ." I paused. "It's very hard to believe my own eyes." I turned my back and switched on the lights. Surely this would send Morgan le Fey back to the land of dreams.

When I turned around, her chair was empty.

Then I heard her skirts rustle right behind me and felt her breath against my cheek. "It is unfortunate that these so-called centuries of science and industry emphasize only what passes for reality, so that a girl like you fears to believe what her dreaming, or even her waking self sees. Is this progress?"

Ms. le Fey, or whoever she was, slipped around the chair and stood right in front of me, beneath the overhead light. She pulled me to my feet. Her touch was as warm and real as the night breeze through the open window.

"Do not your own people say that 'seeing is believing'?" she asked.

What I saw was absolutely beautiful. Creamy white skin, golden eyes, deep auburn hair bound up in a circlet of gold. Except for her gold and jewels and heavy rich gowns, she looked a lot like my mom's side of the family. Tall and willowy.

"A girl like you is afraid to believe what she *Sees*," she whispered.

And that was true, of course. It always had been true.

But how could I trust, really trust, all the things I'd *Seen*—*Seen* even before they happened. It was a curse. It had always been a curse. From the very beginning. I'd had this dream—about Dad and Mom and me in an office piled high with books. A man sat behind a desk, smiling through thick glasses, glasses so thick they made his eyes look like marbles.

"It's for the best, Felicity, dear," he'd said in a smooth, oily voice. "When two people fall out of love with each other, like your parents here, they don't fall out of love with their little girl."

And then just weeks later, there he was. Out of my dreams, at the top of an elevator ride in an office building back home—Dad's lawyer. I was just a little girl then, so little and scared. But from that time on, the dreams had come again and again. Always vivid and real. Like my first glimpse of Maiden's Cottage, six months before Mom even told me we were going to England for her sabbatical.

"You could learn to use those visions to your advantage," Morgan le Fey murmured.

She snapped her fingers, and the lights went out. Except that she was wrapped in some kind of glow, as soft as candlelight. Her cape shimmered with rich embroidery, fine needlework that matched the shapes in my vision. Serpents and dragons—*the shapes in my vision*!

"Very observant." Morgan le Fey smiled. "I am pleased."

I walked to the window and parted the curtains. "So I haven't made you up. Okay, I'll buy that, at least for now. But why are you here?"

"I believe you already know."

I stared out at Glastonbury Tor. The dancing sparkles. The serpents and dragons. I could hear them calling to me, as if I were part of them somehow. As if we were connected. "It's that thing in the box," I said at last. "That golden bowl."

"Cauldron," she corrected. "But call it by its proper name." Morgan le Fey paused and looked out toward the Tor. "Call it the Grail."

The Holy Grail.

"It was uncovered in your world just five days ago," she said.

"Then the vision I had tonight—of Dr. Gildas in the tunnel—was about the past, not the future." I swallowed hard. "That's never happened before."

Morgan le Fey leaned closer. "Did you actually see the Grail?" Her golden eyes glittered in the moonlight.

"Weren't you there?" I asked. "I heard your voice."

"A mere projection." She turned away from the window, her face hidden in shadow. "I am forbidden inside the old catacombs beneath Glastonbury Tor. My Sight will not take there."

"But mine will?"

She didn't answer.

"So you really weren't there at all?" I persisted. "You didn't see that fat priest who looked kind of like Dr. Gildas or the sparkles—"

"The sparkles?" Lady Morgan grabbed my arm. "You saw the Shimmer of Time?"

"I don't know what you're talking about." I pulled away, remembering the nausea, the sicky-sweet smell that had turned my stomach inside out. "I've never had dreams like these, dreams about the past, dreams that could make me throw up."

Morgan le Fey frowned. "A reaction perhaps to my Sight enhancement."

"Your what?"

"An enhancement. To deepen one's Sight. A simple potion of herbs wisely administered." She turned and smiled at me. "Perhaps someday you too will be wise in herb lore. But for now, just a few drops in one of your carbonated beverages or a cup of tea, and what Sights even a primitive Seer such as yourself can *See*!"

"You drugged me!" I gasped, backing away.

"Oh, my dear, there is no cause for alarm." She reached for my hand, but I wouldn't let her touch me. "It is all perfectly natural. A harmonious balance of yarrow, digitalis, nightshade . . ."

But I wasn't listening. All those weeks of dreams and visions, even the waking ones. Now, they made perfect sense. There really wasn't anything wrong with me, anything different. I'd been drugged . . . *drugged*! Maybe even for years and years and years. Since I was a little girl . . .

"Do not be ridiculous." Her voice was suddenly hard and angry. She looked me straight in the eye. "You drank my enhancement no more than thrice these last three weeks."

"I think you'd better go," I said.

"Why must you be so willful?" She pulled me close. Her fingernails dug into my skin. "Will you not trust to my better judgment?"

"Why did you drug my tea?"

"Ah!" She waved her hand in the air. "To *See* if you are suitable."

"Suitable for what?" I asked slowly.

Then her eyes shifted, and she backed away. "Perhaps you are right," she said. "Perhaps I should go now."

And she melted into the wall in a flurry of purple and amber light.

Chapter 4

Vivian Nimuet

*Sir Thomas Malory's retelling of Arthurian literature
has long captured our imaginations. For here we find all the
familiar characters in the Matter of Britain, including those
deeply ambiguous Arthurian women, so essential to the
mystery of Camelot. Why does Malory tell us so little about these
women? Why are they at once evil and good?*
—Dr. Vanessa Jones,
Exploring the Myth of the Grail Keeper

Of course, I couldn't tell Mom about the Holy Grail. I mean, what was I supposed to say? That I'd seen this vision of the Grail because my tea had been drugged by Morgan le Fey?

Right.

Still, I felt this weird kind of responsibility—not to Mom exactly, certainly not to Morgan le Fey. But I had to know more about the Grail. Maybe those dancing serpents and dragons were growing on me. So when Mom came in the next morning, I asked if we could go to the excavation together.

"Certainly not," she said, shoving a thermometer into my mouth. "Dr. Brimmer said she could see you first thing this morning, and we're not making any plans until she gives you a clean bill of health."

Which she did, more or less.

"It's really a question of blood sugar," Dr. Brimmer said, frowning at me over the tops of those little half-glasses people get when they hit thirty or something. "With your low blood pressure, which is certainly within normal range, you really should eat more balanced and nutritious meals."

"Don't worry," Mom promised. "I'll keep my eye on her from now on."

So when I repeated my suggestion about going to the excavation together, Mom said yes—after we'd had a huge (and nutritious) lunch at the Excalibur Café.

It had been a long time since I'd been to an excavation, and I'd forgotten just how boring the whole thing can be. Dozens of people sit around cross-legged or they bend over these string grids that stretch across the ground like graph paper. And all they do is dust away centimeters—no, millimeters—of dirt with dental instruments.

I'm not kidding. *Dental instruments!*

If it's a good day, somebody will find a scrap of pottery or a piece of metal (I'm not talking jewelry here) and everybody will get real excited, and jump around and *oooooohh* and *aaahhh,* their eyes all lit up like a Christmas tree. Then, after a kind of group hug, they all just go back to work again, dusting away one little layer of history at a time. Amazing.

So there I was, stuck among all these sad, boring people who obviously didn't have a life. Nor did they seem to know that Dr. Gildas had already found something absolutely incredible. I mean, nobody was talking about the Grail. And nobody (except Mom and me) seemed to think it was unusual that the whole place was crawling with security guards, who were wearing these really strange jungle camouflage suits.

"There must have been a sale at the army/navy store," Mom muttered under her breath.

"Actually, they call themselves the New Knights of the Round Table." Dr. Frazer, who'd gotten us through the main gate, flashed Mom a quick grin and raised an eyebrow.

"From Glastonbury, no doubt?" Her eyes glittered back. Adults find the dumbest things to flirt about—because that's *exactly* what they were doing.

But Dr. Frazer was a little rusty. "Well," he replied, "the museum couldn't afford real security."

"Most excavations don't need it," I said, and that brought everybody back to earth.

Dr. Frazer frowned and stared off into the distance. Mom checked her watch. "I thought you said he'd see me right away." She nodded toward Dr. Gildas.

He was halfway up the Tor, crouched beside an old woman wearing an enormous sun hat. We'd been waiting over thirty minutes to get beyond what one of the New Knights of the Round Table called "the outer perimeter," where just a handful of volunteers were working. We were nowhere near the main dig by St. Michael's Tower.

Dr. Frazer's frown tightened. "Let's give him another five minutes."

But at just that moment, Dr. Gildas jumped to his feet and his voice rolled down the Tor like thunder. "Nimuet! You incompetent fool!" He waved his arms up and down dramatically. "I want you out of here this afternoon. Do you hear me, woman?"

Simultaneously, all the workers lifted their dental instruments and stared at Dr. Gildas and the old woman, her face completely hidden in the shadows of her hat.

"He's probably staging this whole thing for our benefit," Mom grumbled.

"I wouldn't count on it." Dr. Frazer shook his head. "There's no love lost between Archibald Gildas and Vivian Nimuet."

By this time, Dr. Gildas was jumping up and down like a Jack Russell terrier. Dr. Frazer raced up the path and helped Vivian Nimuet to her feet. Then he turned to Dr. Gildas and pointed down at Mom and me. Instantly, the volunteers hunched back over their string grids.

But Dr. Gildas kept right on looking at us, for what felt like a long time. Finally, he started walking toward us—running really. Then his foot must have hit some loose gravel, because he started sliding down the path. Fast. Dr. Frazer leaped ahead and caught Dr. Gildas by the elbow. That pretty much stopped the slide, but Dr. Gildas yanked his arm away and stomped the rest of the way down the Tor.

"See what you made me do?" he shouted at Mom and me.

"That wasn't our fault," I said.

"I might have broken a limb in that slide." Dr. Gildas took off his sweat-stained straw hat and wiped his head. "What are you doing here anyway, Jones?"

"I was hoping you'd reconsider, let me observe your work, along with Dr. Frazer's." She said this in her best professorial tone, the one she always used when she was trying to impress somebody. But it didn't work.

"This isn't a kindergarten." Dr. Gildas glared first at me, then at Mom. "Get them out of here, Frazer," he snapped.

Mom grabbed his arm. "What gives you the right—"

Dr. Frazer moved between them. "A moment with you, Archie." He led Dr. Gildas a few feet off the path. Mom strode off in the opposite direction.

It was then that I noticed a cluster of canvas tents, across the way in an open field. Headquarters. Excavations like this always had one. And suddenly, an idea popped into my mind. What if that's where Dr. Gildas had hidden the

Grail? I mean, he couldn't keep it buried in that tunnel under the Tor forever. I glanced back at Dr. Gildas, who was still shaking his head furiously. Maybe Mom and I didn't need to get into the excavation after all. If what Morgan le Fey had said the night before was true, my Sight could just *show* me the Grail, couldn't it? I mean, maybe I could summon a vision. True, I'd never done it before. . . . But, what had she said? *You could learn to use those visions to your advantage.*

So I closed my eyes (somehow that seemed like the right thing to do) and concentrated. *Grail, Grail, Grail.* The words beat a rhythm in my temples. A chill ran up my spine; my head felt dizzy and light. I heard a voice—or, at least, I thought I did.

Nice try, it said.

The voice was shaky, tinny. An old woman's voice.

I opened my eyes, and from clear across the Tor, met that old woman's gaze. Vivian Nimuet. She lifted her arm and waved. Surely . . . it couldn't be, I told myself, not another mind reader. Just pure coincidence. I frowned and took a step back—right into Dr. Frazer.

"Pardon me," he said. Then he looked over in Mom's direction and gave her a thumbs-up. She flashed him a big smile, and not five minutes later, the two of them were making their grand tour.

So what about me?

"No casual observers, Felicity," Dr. Frazer had explained. "I'm sorry, but that's Archie's final word—at least for now." So there I was, alone under a big oak tree way down at the base of the Tor, with nothing to do but sit and read.

Which actually didn't seem like a bad idea at the time.

After all, I'd brought along this battered copy of *Le Morte D'Arthur*. I figured that reading about King Arthur's kingdom would put me in the right mood to summon up a vision.

Boy, was I wrong.

Then in all haste came Uther with a great host, and laid siege about the Castle of Terrabil. And there he pitched many pavilions, and there was great war made on both parties, and much people slain.

How does anybody get through language like that?

I rubbed my eyes and laid Sir Thomas aside. A big white cloud passed over the sun, and a cool breeze rustled the leaves in the oak. Mom and Dr. Frazer moved completely out of sight, behind the ruins of the tower. I leaned back against the tree and closed my eyes. The oak leaves whispered overhead.

They whispered and whispered, voices on the wind. Voices I knew. The serpents and dragons were calling to me. My mind reached out to them, and slowly, in sparkles of amber and purple, the Grail took shape. It was faint and misty, its symbols moving across the golden surface in steady ripples. I tried to concentrate, to focus on what I was *Seeing*. But the more I concentrated, the fainter it became. It was slipping away. I couldn't hold it.

My head ached, a slow steady ache right at the temples. *Concentrate. Concentrate.* The patterns shifted, held for a moment.

"You're not going to faint, are you?"

My vision shattered like crystal.

I opened my eyes, and there she was again, that annoying old lady. No wonder Gildas despised her.

She took off her big hat and wiped her forehead with a delicate white handkerchief. "I think when one is older, one feels heat more intensely. But perhaps I've forgotten what it's like to be young. You're sure you're not having a heat stroke, my dear?"

"No, I'm fine." I sighed. "Perfectly normal."

The old lady smoothed her hair, then put her hat back on. Clusters of green and purple plastic grapes spilled over the brim. "Isn't this the most hideous hat you've ever seen?" she whispered. "I only wear it to annoy Archibald."

"You mean Dr. Gildas?"

"Who else? I've known him for years. He was my father's most promising graduate student—until they had a falling out." She rolled up her shirtsleeves like the fairy godmother in Cinderella and held out her hand. "I'm Vivian Nimuet from Seattle, Washington."

"I know." The old woman's grip was strong, steady. "I heard him yelling at you."

"Didn't *everybody*?" Miss Nimuet rolled her eyes. "Petty jealousy, that's all, though Papa's been dead for decades." Miss Nimuet leaned forward and patted my hand. "My father was a brilliant archaeologist, an expert on the pre-Roman Celts. Archibald feels insecure when I'm around."

Mom and Dr. Frazer appeared around the corner of the tower. The wind caught her hair and sent it swirling around her face. She waved at me, then disappeared down the other side of the Tor.

"Your mother, I presume?" Miss Nimuet's golden eyes glimmered.

I nodded.

"You have her hair and height. Is she an archaeologist?"

Normally, I don't get chatty with old ladies. But at just that very moment, Dr. Gildas emerged from one of the canvas tents and strode toward the gate. He scowled in our direction, and I figured that any enemy of his was a friend of mine.

So I told Miss Nimuet all about Mom.

"We're both daughters of scholars!" Miss Nimuet exclaimed, rattling the grapes on her hat. She squeezed my hand. "And since we have so much in common, I'll let you in on a little secret."

She leaned forward and paused dramatically. Too dramatically. I mean, do old ladies ever know important secrets?

Finally, she whispered, "They've found the Holy Grail."

My mouth fell open, and for a long time I just stared at her. At last, I stammered, "But I thought—I thought it was a big secret. Mom doesn't even know!"

"But you knew, didn't you?" Miss Nimuet leaned back, smiling. "I thought you were special. Yes I did. Here. Come with me. Let's nose around Archibald's tent while he's at tea." She sprang to her feet. "The man's an absolute glutton, you know."

I scrambled up and looked around. Mom was completely out of sight, all the New Knights of the Round Table were gossiping by the gate, and most of the volunteers had clustered around the tower, drinking bottled water and sharing granola bars. Apparently, this was the chance I'd been waiting for.

"Hurry up, my dear. We haven't got all day," called Miss Nimuet, striding across the field. I had to run to catch up.

Miss Nimuet pushed open the flap of the biggest tent. "He just wants to make money off the Grail," she confided. "That's really why we quarreled this afternoon."

"But I thought you were a volunteer," I said, stepping into the tent.

It was dark and gloomy inside, smelly too. There were stacks and stacks of papers, folders, and old books, many of them stained with tea, grease, and jam.

"Of course I'm a volunteer," Miss Nimuet was saying. "I volunteered to keep my eye on Archibald. His museum has just about run out of money, so I suspect he's up to no good." She fluttered about a stack of papers behind a packing crate. "And indeed he is!" Miss Nimuet announced. "Look at these." She pointed to a file of newspaper and magazine clippings.

I squinted to read the headlines.

DESIRE FOR SMART BABIES FUELS BIG SALES

SPIRITUAL QUESTS SPUR CONSUMER SPENDING

MUSEUMS CASH IN ON HISTORY

"I don't get it," I said, thinking maybe this hadn't been a good idea. I mean, Miss Nimuet was really weird. Would Mom be like this in thirty years?

"Well heavenly days!" Miss Nimuet sighed and settled into a rickety chair on the opposite side of the tent. "I thought you of all people would understand."

"Why me?"

She just frowned and shoved me another file of clippings about parents who wanted baby Einsteins or people who bought stuff because it made them feel spiritual. My dad's new wife played Mozart for her three-year-old all day and hung crystals from the ceiling. But what did that have to do with the Grail?

Miss Nimuet sorted through another pile. "Look at this!" She heaved a thickly bound stack of paper across the tent. It landed at my feet.

"Royal Regal." I read the name on the cover slowly. "Aren't they that big company that got in trouble recently? Something about low wages for factory workers in Mexico?"

Miss Nimuet looked over her glasses in disgust. "Everyone knows that. See what they're up to now."

So I thumbed through the pages of whatever it was—a recommendation or proposal or something.

"A baby's brain will grow to 70 percent of its adult weight by the age of one," it said. "Companies that offer intellectual products with archetypal appeal can capitalize on this trend."

The whole proposal was filled with statistics, numbers, and charts. Really pointless stuff. Nothing to do with the Grail—or so I thought then.

"Look at this!" cried Miss Nimuet. I ducked as another big notebook sailed across the tent and just cleared my shoulder. Miss Nimuet had amazing strength for an old woman. Good aim too.

This second notebook—or whatever—was even thicker than the first and bound in an expensive-looking cover. *Malory Bede & White.* Sounded like a law firm.

I perched on a shaky old director's chair and slowly turned the first page. "A Proposal for the London Museum of Anglo-Saxon Antiquities." I read the words softly, and they echoed, no kidding, *echoed* through my mind. My hands trembled a little and shivers ran up my spine. And just at the very instant when I closed my eyes, the Grail took shape. Clear. Sharp. Perfect.

The vision held. I could see the cauldron beautifully, almost as if I was holding it in my own two hands. But where was it? Where had Gildas hidden it? I couldn't tell, though I tried and tried and tried to *See.* All that came to me was the cauldron itself.

Then something was shaking me, shaking me hard. The vision of the Grail fizzled and popped in a flurry of light—all amber and purple.

"Put that away." It was Miss Nimuet. "We've already stayed here too long." And suddenly, the Grail was gone.

She pulled me to my feet. The proposal dropped with a dull thud.

"Hurry!" Miss Nimuet repeated. "A good spy never gets caught." Already her voice sounded far away, and I realized I was alone inside the tent.

The proposal rested in a mound of sawdust. Should I take it? In all this clutter, would Dr. Gildas even miss it?

"Felicity!" Miss Nimuet's voice was insistent.

Don't arouse suspicion.

My voice. My inner voice. The one I was learning to trust.

So I tried to place the proposal back where Miss Nimuet had found it, then followed her out into the sunshine.

Chapter 5

At Chalice Well

*It is part of the oral tradition here, that the spring that fills
Chalice Well has magical properties. Indeed, the old wives of Somerset
say that if you drink its rusty red waters, then stare into the stream
itself, you will see visions.*
—Dr. Merlin Nimuet,
Folkways of the Somerset Country

I caught up with Miss Nimuet by the gate to the
Chalice Well garden. "Fortunately, I have a
plan," she was saying, as if I'd been behind her
all along. "I happen to know someone at Malory
Bede and White." She held up her pass and the
garden attendant waved us through.

"So, what's your plan?" I asked.

"You'll infiltrate their offices, of course," she
answered, striding past clumps of four-o'clocks
and lilies. "As a student intern."

"Wait a minute," I said, blocking her path.
"I'm no intern and I'm no spy."

Miss Nimuet pushed back her sun hat. The grapes on the brim jangled unpleasantly. "Well, blow me down! I thought you had more spunk. Besides, who wouldn't want an internship with MBW?"

"What is it? A bunch of lawyers?"

"An advertising agency." Miss Nimuet frowned. "What else could it be?" She brushed past me, her face flushed. No wonder Dr. Gildas found her so irritating.

And that gave me an idea. So I turned around and started back for Dr. Gildas's tent. Who needed an internship when that MBW proposal was there for the taking? But I didn't get very far.

MBW. MBW.

Inside my head, I was seeing the cover of that proposal. The letters *MBW* came flying off the page, buzzing and darting at me like hungry mosquitoes after dark. Then I saw a gleam of gold, a flash of ruby. I crumpled as a wave of nausea hit me hard—the same sickness, the very same I'd had in that tunnel. You know, when Morgan le Fey drugged me.

"You look extremely unwell." Miss Nimuet was suddenly at my side. "Come with me, my dear."

I didn't have the strength to argue. Slowly, she turned and led me toward the deep shade at the back of the garden, toward Chalice Well. And the closer I got to the well, the better I felt. Still, I couldn't help wondering if I'd been drugged again. But who could have done it? And when? I hadn't had anything to drink since the Excalibur Café.

"Here we are," Miss Nimuet said softly. "Now you sit right here." She guided me toward the well, so shady and cool. I sank down on a bench and stared into the depths of the well. I'd been there before with Mom, but the well had been closed up, sealed by an ornate bronze cover.

"Put your head between your knees, and I'll get you a drink of water."

"I don't want anything to drink!" I said, wondering how Miss Nimuet had managed to open the well.

"Didn't I tell you to put your head down?" She gently pushed my head toward my knees.

I really can't explain what happened next. One minute she was fumbling with a collapsible plastic cup, and then . . . Everything went all purple and golden, and I was rushing through a tunnel of light with voices, lots of whispering voices. Then, just as suddenly, I was standing in daylight by this spring, a cool babbling spring, and Miss Nimuet was handing me that collapsible cup.

"You're unwell, my dear," she said, shoving the cup under my nose. "Drink from this spring water."

I took the cup and looked around. I mean, everything seemed different. The air. The sky. The place. Where was the well, the carefully tended garden? Why did I feel so dizzy and weak? Not sick, mind you. *Dizzy and weak!*

"Drink, Felicity," she ordered.

Now I know what you're thinking. Obviously, given the circumstances, I shouldn't drink the water. I mean, if I hadn't been drugged before, this was the perfect opportunity. But honestly, I don't know what got into me. The cup felt so cool and soothing in my hand. The water, or whatever it was, looked beautiful—a pale, rusty pink. And Miss Nimuet sounded so persuasive.

So I drank every last drop of that stuff. It tasted sweet and pure, like water *should* taste but never does. It cleared my head, steadied my legs.

Then, just when I'd started to get my bearings, when I *knew* the Chalice Well garden wasn't anywhere in the neighborhood and that maybe, just maybe, I wasn't where I thought I was, I felt myself slipping into darkness.

Breathe deeply and concentrate on what you See, somebody was saying. Miss Nimuet or Morgan le Fey—I wasn't sure. *What you seek will come.*

So I opened my eyes, and found myself staring down at the swirling, bubbling waters of the spring. Beneath the surface, I saw the Grail. Perfectly—down to every detail of every one of those serpents and dragons etched on its surface. And at its center, something I hadn't seen before—the image of a goddess rising from a pool of water, arms outstretched, reaching toward the sky. Did she call my name? I plunged both hands into the stream. Surely, I could just lift the Grail whole right out of the water.

Then I realized it wasn't in the stream at all. It was packed away somewhere, inside something hard and smooth. Something moving fast. Maybe over a highway. Yes, yes. It was moving. In a van. A black van with red lettering on its side. Dr. Gildas had the Grail in his van and was taking it to London that very instant!

I shook off the vision and reached for Miss Nimuet. But where was she? And why was I back in the tunnel of voices with all those lights—those purple and golden lights . . .

"Has she fainted again?"

It was Mom, her voice all panicked and shrill. "Somebody call an ambulance!"

"I need to get to London." My voice came out all wrong.

"Oh, my god!" Mom cried. "She's delirious!"

I tugged on Mom's sleeve. "No. You don't understand," I whispered. "London. They have a job for me. At MBW."

Miss Nimuet peered over Mom's shoulder. "There. You see. I knew she'd come to her senses."

And just for an instant, I thought I saw a trail of purple and amber lights swirling around her hat.

Chapter 6

Half-Remembered Secrets

*Glastonbury Tor has long stood at a kind of
mythological crossroads for both Celtic and
Christian cultures. Its history is so closely
linked to mythology that one must wonder
if we, as mere historians, can ever unravel
its secrets.*
—Dr. Ian Frazer,
"The Glastonbury Myths,"
Journal of Modern Mythological Exploration

I tried to sit up, but Mom firmly pressed my
shoulders back against the ground. "Oh, no you
don't. You're not going anywhere until we get an
ambulance here."

"I don't need an ambulance. I'm just fine!"

"Give the girl some air, Vanessa!"

At last, the voice of reason—and it belonged
to Dr. Frazer. I expected an argument from Mom,
but she just leaned back and sighed.

"Why don't you let me drive the two of you
home in my Cruiser?" he continued. "Felicity

can stretch out in the backseat. Then call your doctor if you like."

So that's what we did. Except for calling the doctor. Miss Nimuet saw to that. "Too much sun, Dr. Jones. That's all there is to it," she'd said, as we were about to pull away. "But do have Felicity tell you all about the little trip she needs to make to London. Believe me, it will do you both a world of good."

As she'd waved good-bye, the grapes on the brim of her hat bobbled like marbles, sending out one last puff of sparkles. This time, there was no doubt about it. But I guess Mom was too busy staring at me to notice.

"So you weren't delirious when you asked to go to London." Mom frowned. "I guess I should be relieved. But why London?"

We were back at Maiden's Cottage, sitting on the terrace. Mom had brewed some really strong tea and forced me to drink my cup dry. It was bitter and dark and smelled kind of like mothballs. By this time, I was beginning to get suspicious any time anybody gave me something to drink. But I had no choice, and besides, Dr. Frazer was drinking the same stuff—and he was on his second cup.

Mom nudged my arm. "Why London?" She paused and her fingers dug into my arm. "You didn't stage all this just to get away from Glastonbury? Because if you did . . ."

Dr. Frazer got to his feet, and Mom's voice broke off.

"Perhaps I should be going now," he said.

"Please don't."

Mom and I said it together, at exactly the same time. Which was really bizarre. I mean, how often do you and your mom think alike, much less talk alike? Well, it cleared the air and we both kind of laughed. So did Dr. Frazer.

Mom settled back in her chair. "It's been a disappointing day all around." She touched my cheek. "I have a daughter who faints dead away at the drop of a hat—and I still don't know any more about this thing you've found up on the Tor." She frowned at Dr. Frazer, then walked to the edge of the terrace. It was almost dark, but you could see the lopsided shape of the Tor against the sky. "Still," she said, almost whispering, "I can't help feeling that I was very close to something important, maybe even powerful."

Which made me wonder if somehow, some way, Mom had sensed the Grail too.

That's when the phone rang. I dashed into the front hall and picked up the receiver. "Hello," I said.

"Jones, is that you?"

Before I could answer, the voice went on, pushy and smug. "This is Archibald Gildas. I've changed my mind. From now on, I'm giving you unlimited access to the Tor. It's the least I can do."

"It certainly is the least you can do!" I shouted back. "There's nothing there anymore!" But he'd already hung up.

Mom, however, had heard the whole thing. So had Dr. Frazer.

"What are you talking about, Felicity?" Mom's voice was cold. She took the phone from my hands and listened to the silence on the other end. "Who was that?"

"Dr. Gildas." I paused. "He said you can work at the Tor. No restrictions."

"It's about time," she said slowly. "But there's more, isn't there? Do you know something I don't know?"

Dr. Frazer took the phone from Mom and gently put it back in place. "I think you'd both better come with me. Right now."

He steered the car up to the excavation's main gate and rolled down his window. The security guard, another one of those New Knights of the Round Table, flashed a light on Dr. Frazer's ID badge, then into the Cruiser. For half a second, I felt like a spy in an old World War II movie.

"Dr. Jones and her daughter," Dr. Frazer said. "Dr. Gildas cleared them tonight."

The Knight went back to his station, pulled out a metal clipboard, and flashed his light down what must have been a list or something. Then he came back. "Okay. Proceed."

Dr. Frazer parked the Cruiser, then Mom and I followed him down to Dr. Gildas's tent, a pale, lumpy shadow in the darkness. The moon sailed over the top of the Tor, and the wind whispered through the trees. The place felt different at night. Silent and old and full of half-remembered secrets.

Then we were inside the tent. Dr. Frazer struck a match and lighted a Coleman lantern hanging from the center post.

It was the lantern from my vision. You know, the one where I saw Dr. Gildas in the passageway, holding a lantern—that lantern—at the very moment when he'd found the Grail. I backed away. Great shadowy shapes danced against the canvas walls. *Please, please. Not now. No Grail creatures!*

"You're not going to faint again, are you?" Mom squinted at me hard.

"I'm fine. Really."

She wrinkled her nose. "The smell in here's enough to make anyone swoon. What a pig!" She bent to pick up a fat bound notebook at her feet.

"Malory Bede and White," I whispered. "May I see that?"

But Mom was already moving across the tent to a dark corner where Dr. Frazer was kneeling by a metal safe. A digital lock glowed red against the shadows. Slowly, Dr. Frazer punched in the combination and the door swung open.

The safe was empty.

Dr. Frazer cursed under his breath. "I never should have trusted him."

Mom knelt by the empty safe. "I want the truth and I want it now."

There was a long, long pause. Scary, silent, heavy. Dr. Frazer stroked his beard and stared into the empty safe.

Finally, he said, "We may have found the Holy Grail."

Chapter 7

A Loathsome Profession

*The market is ripe for reproductions of antiquities,
particularly those with perceived mystical or spiritual
qualities.*
—*A Proposal for the London Museum of
Anglo-Saxon Antiquities, Malory Bede & White*

We may have found the Holy Grail.

You would have thought a bolt of lightning, a ring of fire, or at least a handful of sparkles would have flashed through the tent. Something. But no. Dr. Frazer just sat there with this worried look on his face, and Mom just watched him.

"It's extraordinary, Vanessa," Dr. Frazer said at last. "What we found here conforms to everything we know about Celtic ornamentation—only finer." He paused. "And you were right about the Grail. It's undoubtedly Celtic, perhaps inscribed to the Lady of the Lake."

I'd expected Mom would explode like a case of Fourth of July fireworks. I mean, after all those years of work, to find out—and find out like this, with an empty safe staring her in the face. But she just said, "You examined it thoroughly then?"

Dr. Frazer shook his head. "Only once, and under tight supervision from Archie and his marketing partner. It was highly irregular. Couldn't even see the Grail until he mumbled some kind of incantation over it."

I remembered that burned scrap of paper in the tunnel, that voice: *Use the charm.* What could that mean? A charm, an incantation?

"How do you know it's the real thing?" Mom was saying.

Then Dr. Frazer started telling us about the goddess at the center of the cauldron, the one I'd *Seen,* rising from that lake or whatever. He moved closer to us, held the lantern high. His eyes had this kind of passion, like a fire burning deep down inside. And as strange as this sounds, I knew *exactly* how he felt. I mean, those Grail creatures—and their goddess—they grab you somehow and won't let go.

Even Mom seemed convinced, just from Dr. Frazer's description. Her eyes got all misty. "I knew, just *knew* all along. It was like a vision. . . ." She held out her arms to me, and we hugged each other. Tight. Then Mom pulled

away and I could tell she was embarrassed—
almost breaking down like that in front of somebody who was practically a stranger.

"So what do we do next?" she asked.

Dr. Frazer lowered the lantern and looked at
me. "Maybe we should ask your daughter. She
seems to know more about this than either one
of us."

There's nothing there anymore.

That's what I'd said on the phone to Gildas—
and unfortunately Dr. Frazer remembered.

Mom folded her arms and raised an eyebrow.
"What do you know about this, Felicity?"

I glanced at the safe. "I think Dr. Gildas took
the Grail to London." Which was the truth.
Obviously.

"How do you know?"

Her voice was definitely building toward an
explosion. I mean, Mom could forgive Dr. Frazer
for keeping the Grail a secret, but not her own
daughter. Basic Mom psychology, right? So I had
to think fast.

"I just put two and two together," I said, still
staring at the safe. "I saw him drive away in that
black and red van of his this afternoon. And
then, on the phone—he told me he was calling
from London."

A little white lie—but it diffused Mom's fireworks. Almost.

Because just as Dr. Frazer extinguished the lantern and headed outside, Mom said, "An odd coincidence, isn't it? All that mumbo jumbo about London this afternoon." She paused, looked me straight in the eyes, then lifted the flap and slipped outside.

I started after her when my foot hit something solid and sent it skittering across the tent, through the doorway. It landed in a puff of purple and amber lights just behind Mom. The MBW notebook.

Mom turned as I picked it up. "What's that?" she asked.

"I think it's a proposal." A few sparkles spilled out between the covers and flickered into nothingness.

"Let me see."

I handed it to Mom, and she started thumbing through the pages; they glowed a soft amber and purple. Mom didn't seem to notice.

Neither did Dr. Frazer. But once he saw the name Malory Bede & White on the cover, he said, "Archie's partner is with MBW. Let's take this with us."

So I stuck it in the bottom of my backpack to make sure a bunch of sparkles wouldn't shoot out and set off security. The guard waved us through and Dr. Frazer gunned the Cruiser back to Maiden's Cottage. Then we started reading.

The MBW notebook was all about the Grail. Not its past. But its future—as some kind of product from Royal Regal. You know, like those Queen Nefertiti Christmas ornaments or the Michelangelo's *David* refrigerator magnets. Miss Nimuet was right: Dr. Gildas and his museum planned to make loads of money off the Grail.

"How can he live with himself?" Mom cried. "Selling cheap reproductions of something as magnificent as the Grail." She tossed the MBW proposal over to Dr. Frazer, and a burst of sparkles glittered across the carpet. Mom took off her glasses and rubbed her eyes. "I wonder if I need bifocals."

Which made me wonder . . . Was Mom seeing sparkles after all?

"You're tired, that's all," Dr. Frazer replied, as the wall clock at Maiden's Cottage struck two.

I reached for the proposal, and those glittery things burst off the page like dozens of tiny comets. They had to be some kind of clue. Think about it a minute. First, they were with the Grail, then Morgan le Fey, then (for whatever reason) with Miss Nimuet. And here they were again—all over that proposal. Dr. Gildas's marketing partner maybe?

"Gildas is scum," Mom said as she reached for a cup of decaf. "The Grail is a cultural icon."

Okay, okay. That I could believe.

But why should a few harmless reproductions be that dangerous? Why get all bent out of shape about it? I got my answer, more or less—from Dr. Frazer. He ran his hands through his hair and said, "This will kill the power of the Grail. The legend will wither and die."

The legend will die.

Could that be it? All those old stories would die off if the world were flooded with plastic Grails. Morgan le Fey, King Arthur, Camelot—everything would just fade away like that pet rock craze from the '70s we'd studied in Popular Culture last year. But even if it did, so what? Which made me ask, "Why does any of this really matter?"

Mom and Dr. Frazer stared at me like I was brain dead. "The Grail's a symbol of inspiration and creativity," Mom said in her English professor voice. "A source of plenty that feeds and sustains the human imagination."

Dr. Frazer walked to the window and stared out toward Glastonbury Tor. His voice was quiet and low, scary even. "But it was far more than a symbol to the ancient Celts. They believed in its power absolutely. Its destruction would make the world a wasteland."

I shivered. Because it sounded like Dr. Frazer believed that himself. And somehow, so did I.

"Don't be melodramatic, Ian." Mom frowned. "You're starting to sound like the locals. Next thing I know, you'll be running your own magic crystal business." She picked up their cups and carried them out to the kitchen for a refill. Slowly, Dr. Frazer turned around, and our eyes met.

He's hiding something!

Don't ask me how, but I just knew it, felt it. Something about the Grail, something about what he *knew*! After all, Dr. Frazer had seen the real thing, maybe even touched it. What were my measly little visions compared to all that? Dr. Frazer looked away quickly, almost like he'd blurted out some big secret. Then he followed Mom into the kitchen.

I shoved the MBW proposal back on the coffee table, and a cloud of amber sparkles swirled into shape. And this time, they didn't disappear. They just kept swirling. I leaned forward.

They shifted color!

Now they were red, bloodred.

And they began to form a distinct shape. A head like a lizard, horns like a ram, then wings, legs, talons . . . The dragon from the ring I'd seen in those visions—down in the tunnel! That awful smell, too sweet to breathe, filled the room, and a wave of sickness broke over me again—only stronger than ever before. Really, really strong.

The dragon broke apart and dissolved like images on a screen saver. I dashed out to the terrace. I held my stomach tight, refusing to be sick. I don't know about you, but I hate being sick worse than anything. That's where Mom found me.

"You'll catch pneumonia out here, Felicity. Come back inside," she said.

"The red dragon," I mumbled. "What does it mean?"

"Is there something in the proposal about the Pendragon?" Mom asked, guiding me back inside.

"The Pendragon?" A sip of tea started to settle my stomach.

"Arthur's family symbol," explained Dr. Frazer. "It means head dragon or leader."

"So," I said slowly, almost afraid of what I was saying, "somebody who wore a Pendragon ring would be related to King Arthur?"

"Where did you see anything about jewelry?" Mom asked, reaching for the proposal. Not a single sparkle escaped, not even when she thumbed through the pages. "The only Pendragon I see in the whole manuscript is right here—on the title page."

I looked over Mom's shoulder—and she was right. There it was, the Pendragon, right above the Malory Bede & White logo.

"What do you know about this advertising agency?" Dr. Frazer asked suddenly.

And then I knew. That *was* the connection. The person wearing the Pendragon ring in my visions had to be at Malory Bede & White, had to be Dr. Gildas's partner. That's why the Pendragon was on the title page!

"Advertising." Mom shook her head. "It's so immoral—making people buy things they don't really need. A loathsome profession."

"Nevertheless," Dr. Frazer's eyes narrowed, "they've apparently persuaded Archie to go along with this scheme." He picked up the proposal. "We'd better start learning about this agency. Now." Again his eyes met mine. Again I felt that he wasn't telling us everything he knew—or that maybe he was worried about something.

But he gave me an easy opening, because no matter what all this was *really* about, MBW held all the cards. Wasn't that what Miss Nimuet had been trying to tell me? So I said, "He's right, Mom."

I paused, almost scared to go on. I mean, who wants to come face to face with a villain who wears dragon jewelry and makes you want to throw up? But did I have a choice? "There's something I've been meaning to tell you all night . . . about this London thing."

"Okay." Mom plopped onto the couch.

"Miss Nimuet asked me to apply for an internship at Malory Bede and White—in London. I think I should do it."

I waited for Mom to explode, but she didn't. Instead she sat really still, her coffee cup poised mid-sip, her eyes all trancey.

It was like a vision. . . .

Mom's words . . . Is that how she'd written all those books about King Arthur? Was she having some kind of vision at that very moment?

Then Mom just snapped back to reality like she'd never been gone. She finished her coffee and said, "So do I. Let's go to London."

Chapter 8

Something Terrible Had Happened. . . .

And when the Holy Grail had been borne through the hall, then the
holy vessel departed suddenly, that they wist not where it became. . . .
—Sir Thomas Malory,
Le Morte D'Arthur

I pressed my head against the window and watched the village of Glastonbury slip away. The bus was noisy, crowded, uncomfortable. Merlin was yowling from inside the picnic basket under my feet. Mom was smashed in beside me, taking notes on some manuscript Dr. Frazer had loaned her. Don't ask me how Mom could do it: read, concentrate, and write in a noisy, swaying, crowded bus with a freaked-out cat. But I've known her to take notes during an earthquake. Really. At some medievalist convention in L.A. Halfway into the quake before Mom even noticed what was happening . . .

Anyway, this whole trip had come together like magic. Miss Nimuet set everything up, from loaning us her father's old flat in London to getting me an interview at Malory Bede & White.

"Crystal DuLac. She's the one managing interns this summer," Miss Nimuet had explained. "Well actually, there's only one, and he quit last week."

"Why did he quit?" I'd asked.

"Who knows? Couldn't stomach the work, I guess."

Well, that wasn't reassuring. Neither was the next thing she said.

"Now, I must warn you. Crystal is . . ." Miss Nimuet frowned. "Well, there's just no way around it. Crystal is eccentric—to say the least."

If Miss Nimuet thought this Crystal was eccentric, well, you can imagine how that made me feel.

Across the aisle, a little girl tipped over a whole can of Coke, and instead of cleaning it up, her mom was yelling at her. And the girl's brother was laughing and telling her what a spaz she was.

I turned away and tried to concentrate on the passing scenery. If I remembered right, we were just about to Stonehenge, where the highway widened and straightened out a little. But it had started raining—hard—and I couldn't be sure. Besides, I had other things on my mind. For example: Maybe that intern had quit because of Crystal DuLac. And what kind of name was that anyway—Crystal DuLac? It had to be a made-up name, invented. By someone eccentric? Maybe. Or maybe by a Time traveler who wore sickening perfume and a Pendragon ring . . .

Suddenly, the bus lurched forward, then jerked to a stop. I reached out to steady myself, but we were already moving again. Sort of. Moving ahead but shaking. Shaking. Rattling. Jingling. Like that L.A. earthquake. Only worse—lots worse.

I glanced at Mom. But she wasn't there! All I could see was a shimmering cluster of purple and amber lights. In every direction—no matter which way I turned! I reached out to touch them. The lights swirled over my hand and ran up my arm. I shook them off, but then these tingles starting shooting up my arm like little electric shocks! Before long, I was feeling them everywhere—my arms, my legs, my back, my neck.

And the tingles didn't go away, not even when the lights thinned out, so I could almost see through them—shapes moving beyond a glowing wall. I squinted really hard. And there was Mom. But she was different somehow. Thinner, older. Her hair cut short. A little boy with her, maybe eight or nine—I don't know. He was skinny and sickly looking with a head full of wavy, black hair.

The next thing I knew, it was gone. The boy. Mom. The tingles. The wall of lights. The shaking. Everything. And Mom was sitting next to me, looking the way she always does with her red hair braided across the top of her head.

"Did you feel that?" she said breathlessly.

But before I could say anything, Mom glanced away. "Of course not. No one did." She took off her glasses and sighed. "I'm seeing things, losing my balance—must be middle age."

Okay. So maybe I should have asked Mom what she'd seen, what she'd felt. And we both might have guessed right then what was happening to us. But it wasn't that easy. I mean, maybe Mom *did* need a new pair of glasses. Maybe the bus *had* hit a rough spot in the road. And as we all know, by this time I could see those purple and amber lights whenever I just *thought* about them. Besides, nobody else had even noticed. The little girl across from us was still crying, her mom was still yelling, her brother was still laughing, and Coke was gushing down the aisle like some kind of flash flood. So why make a big deal out of nothing?

Merlin had stopped yowling. I reached into the picnic basket, scooped him up, and held him close. He usually had this kind of calming effect on me, you know? But not this time. I couldn't shake this feeling that something terrible had happened—or might be happening, or was going to happen. Even after the rest of our trip came off without a hitch.

Miss Nimuet's old bedroom in her father's London flat was a small, stuffy room tucked up under the eaves on the top floor of a building that must have been built in 1890 or something. Don't get me wrong. It was charming, with an angled roof and quaint old furniture. But if I didn't watch where I was going, I'd bang my head on the ceiling. And I don't think the window had been opened in decades. It took me forever to get it open.

Mom had gone to bed early in Dr. Nimuet's old bedroom and Merlin refused to leave his picnic basket in the kitchen. So I was alone—except for all those nagging little fears that just wouldn't go away. First, I couldn't get rid of that sense of foreboding—like (I know this sounds sick) but like someone in your family had just died or found out they had an incurable disease. Second, there was Crystal DuLac. And third, there was the interview—with Crystal DuLac. What if I threw up all over her Pendragon ring? Finally, about midnight, I turned out the light and tried to sleep.

It wasn't easy. Neon lights from the theater across the street flashed through the darkness. Red. Green. Yellow. White. Red. Green. Yellow. White. Over and over and over again. Just when I'd gotten used to their pattern, when I thought the rhythm of those lights would push me into sleep, everything went gray. The lights went out.

I was back on the bus again.

And just like before, there was this terrific jolt, and a wall of purple and amber sparkles surrounded me. But this time, there was a rushing wind hurling me through a tunnel of darkness. Voices whispered past. Shadowy shapes slipped by. I could just make out the face of that raven-haired boy. But the wind drove me past him, toward a golden light far, far away.

And then I was floating, way up high. Flying maybe. It was as if I'd always been able to fly— like a kestrel. Fast but graceful.

Below me were crowds of people gathered in a gigantic stone building. A building kind of like a church—or a castle. And the people gathered there were wearing beautiful, shining tunics, gowns, and capes—or was it just the light that made everything glow? A pure, radiant, glowing light that filled the hall with soft shimmers of purple and amber.

It was the Grail! That was the source of the light.

I could see the etchings, those magical creatures on its surface, moving around and around. They called to me, but I couldn't make out their words. And the goddess was singing a clear, sweet, perfect song. The light grew brighter— clean and fierce and white. Still, I'd never felt happier, more joyful. Because despite all that light, despite its blinding brightness, I could see!

What kind of magic is this? my inner voice cried out.

Do you not know? another voice answered. Morgan le Fey's voice. *Behold the magic of the Grail.*

And suddenly, there she was. Morgan le Fey.

The Grail hovered over her uplifted hands. Another woman stood at her side, and she smiled up at me—just as the Grail sent out another wondrous burst of light. Why was her smile so familiar?

At the back of the hall, where the light was as soft as a summer day, the crowd parted. A big man in a purple cloak and a slim woman with golden hair moved through all those masses of people—toward Morgan le Fey, her assistant, and the glowing, shining Grail. It soared higher and higher, as bright as the sun. The Grail creatures began to sing with the goddess, and almost, *almost* I could understand the words to their song.

Then the hall went gray—as gray as twilight.

Instantly, silently, a group of men surrounded the tall man and the woman at his side. Were they being protected or attacked? I wasn't sure. Because there was a sudden movement behind Morgan le Fey, a knife at her throat, a jeweled hand pulling her arms down, wrapping them behind her back. The Grail fell, crashing against the floor. The hall went dark.

But somehow, I could still *See*!

Couldn't anybody else? Had they all gone blind? Because there was that fat priest—the one who looked like Dr. Gildas—and he was scrambling toward Morgan le Fey. Nobody stopped him, not even when he kneeled by the Grail and started reaching for it. His lips were moving and his hands made an odd, jerky motion—*a charm against magic,* my inner voice said.

Morgan le Fey struggled against the arms gripping her tight. I squinted through the darkness. Who held her captive? Was it a man or a woman? I couldn't tell. It was like shadows or a mist or something shrouded everything about that person, except the arms—and hands. For in that instant, I saw the gleaming Pendragon ring.

The fat priest locked the Grail away in a bronze box and called out something in a language I couldn't understand. The arms pushed Morgan le Fey to the floor, and the smell of that nauseating perfume wafted toward me like poison gas. I gagged, sickened, felt myself falling. Falling fast!

I tried to scream, but nothing came out. Falling, falling, falling!

Then I was awake, and Morgan le Fey was leaning against my bed, looking as sick as I felt.

Chapter 9

A Magic Crafted Only for the Wearer

Highly embellished torques or neck bands, found at selected sites in the British Isles, may have been crafted for a select few within Celtic society and worn only for important civic or ritual functions. Could the early Celts have believed such jewelry exerted magical properties?
—Dr. Ian Frazer,
Archaeological Perspectives on the Ancient Celts

"Are you okay?" I asked, breathing in great gulps of fresh air.

Morgan le Fey drew herself up very tall, but as she reached her full height, she had to steady herself against the headboard.

"What do you think?" she said, her voice raspy and low. Her hands were shaking—no, her whole body was shaking, shivering really. "Give me that blanket," she ordered, nodding toward an afghan at the bottom of the bed.

74

I draped it over her shoulders. "You better lie down." My sickness had passed, but hers obviously hadn't.

Morgan le Fey shook her head, but drew the afghan closer. "A rough crossing this time." The cloud of sparkles around her gown dimmed, and for an instant, she seemed almost transparent. Wisps of gray light filtered in through the bedroom window, but even in that dim light, I saw it: a dark bruise against the white of her throat. From that hand holding the knife?

"You were there," she said, answering my thought the way she always did. "You saw how I got this." She bent over suddenly, clutching her stomach—and it was like I could sense her pain without really feeling it—a violent, churning nausea.

"You really ought to lie down," I said again.

But she shook me off. "Are you blind to the truth?" Her words came out slowly, between waves of sickness. "Can you not see, do you not know? The Grail has been lost—taken from me."

I was suddenly cold. Shivering cold. My nightmare, or whatever, was starting to make sense. "A conspiracy," I said slowly. "Between the priest who looks like Dr. Gildas and the person who wears that ring. The one who held that knife to your throat!"

Morgan le Fey started to cough, gag really—like she had the dry heaves.

"We need to get you to the bathroom." I grabbed her shoulders, and there it was again: that sickening perfume. It clung to her clothes like cigarette smoke.

Faint as it was, the smell got to me. Again. I staggered to the window for another dose of fresh air. But Morgan le Fey collapsed on the edge of the bed.

The fresh air settled my stomach and maybe even cleared my head. Because as I turned to help her, a really scary idea popped into my mind: that the person with the Pendragon ring had to be one pretty powerful character, maybe even more powerful than Morgan le Fey herself.

"No one is more powerful than I!" she cried, as the afghan fell from her shoulders. "No one."

Well, that may have been what *she* believed, but the facts pointed in the opposite direction.

"I hear what you are thinking, Felicity Jones," Morgan le Fey gasped. "But I envisioned this conspiracy, even as I fought to prevent it. As for this illness, it is but a temporary inconvenience."

Then she reached into the folds of her gown and took out a little clay vial. I backed away; I'd already had enough of her magic potions. But this time, she drank it herself.

"For an unsettled stomach," she said, holding the vial out to me. "Perhaps you, too, are in need of its properties."

I pushed the vial away. "What is it about that smell? Why does it make people sick?"

Morgan le Fey's eyes narrowed. "I believe most people find its fragrance attractive. But on all of us, save one, it works as a repellent."

Looking back on things, there are two questions I should have pursued here. But I could only focus on one—that ominous phrase, *all of us*. What did that mean?

Morgan le Fey looked me square in the face. "We who are Keepers of the Grail. We who have the power to take it back!"

And then I wished I hadn't even thought the question. *We who are Keepers of the Grail.* Did that mean I was like Morgan le Fey? A sorceress? A witch?

No way. *No way!*

The stomach potion must have worked its magic because Morgan le Fey jumped to her feet. *How can you deny your destiny!*

I swear, I heard her as plain as day. So I replied, *I don't believe in destiny!*

But I hadn't really replied. And I hadn't really heard Morgan le Fey at all. I mean, for the first time, I'd heard one of her *thoughts*—and answered, just by thinking. And before I knew it, before Morgan le Fey knew it, I heard her next thought too.

The maid's powers are growing. He will know her.

My mind went blank. So did Morgan le Fey's. And we just sat there, staring at each other. The pale gray nighttime light of London poured through the window, making a dim and colorless cave of Miss Nimuet's old room. Everything was gray, everything was shadow.

I was a sorceress. I was a witch.

I sent out another thought, but Morgan le Fey's mind was a thick fog. This time, I couldn't find my way through.

"You see, you still have much to learn, little Grail Keeper." Morgan le Fey threw back her head and laughed. "Such an innocent you are, such a child of your time." She touched my hair. "Perhaps there is nothing to fear after all. Still, one cannot be too careful. . . ."

Then she reached into her gown again. I expected another vial, some potion to bring on a trance, to help me *See* my destiny—or at least, the wearer of the Pendragon ring. Instead, Morgan le Fey took out a heavy silver necklace. A choker, really. Set with amber stones.

"This was made for you," she said. "A gift from Avalon."

The choker fell into my hands. It was cold and heavy, but even in all that gloom, the amber glowed warm and golden. The necklace looked familiar somehow, like it was part of one of those childhood memories, you know the kind—just an image or a flash, maybe even a dream from when you were so tiny you didn't have words for anything yet. Well, that's what it felt like, looking at that necklace. And it scared me a little.

No. It scared me a lot.

"It has its own magic," Morgan le Fey continued. "A magic crafted only for its wearer."

I dropped the necklace on the bed. "I don't want your magic. I don't want to *be* magic!"

Morgan le Fey gave me one of her half smiles, and I heard what she was thinking.

You cannot fight what you are. But you will not be what you are unless you fight.

What are you talking about? I thought back.

Then my mind flashed on to the bus—to that strange image of the dark-haired boy and Mom, looking tired and old. All of that had to be related somehow. But how?

Answer me! my mind cried out. *What's this really about?*

And then—I'm not sure whether I read her thoughts or what—but Morgan le Fey told me this: *Your fate—and your mother's—are linked to the Grail.*

The next thing I knew, she'd lifted her arms and a dusting of lights was swirling up from the hem of her gown. "Wear the necklace, Felicity, for your own protection."

"Protection from what?"

The swirl of lights grew brighter, higher, thicker. And for the first time, I realized that they formed a kind of doorway. Morgan le Fey stepped inside.

I wanted to rush after her, to push through and find the truth. But the sparkles flickered out, and all I was left with was that witchy-looking necklace, its amber stones glowing in the dark like hot coals.

Chapter 10

Realer Than Real

If you must hire another intern to meet
this year's public service objectives, put him
to work filing. Deny all access to information
about the Grail.
—Geoffrey Mordreaut,
MBW e-mail to Crystal DuLac

"So Auntie Nim sent you," she said. She being Ms. Crystal DuLac.

I searched my brain trying to figure out what she was talking about, while she looked over the tops of her teeny, tiny little wire-framed glasses and smiled.

"You probably call her Vivian or Miss Nimuet," she said.

"Oh, right." I nodded and tried to think of what to say next. It was hard to focus because this Crystal DuLac wasn't at all like I'd imagined. She had heaps of red hair—darker than Mom's or mine—tied up with a gypsy scarf, and her earrings made this annoying jingle every time she tilted her head. The only good news: She wasn't wearing a Pendragon ring.

"But she's not really your aunt," I said finally. "Miss Nimuet, I mean."

"Oh, heavens no. She and her father had a flat in my building, that's all—when I was a little girl." She reached for a file. How she kept all those bracelets from snagging her racy little crocheted dress was beyond me.

"It's a matter of coordination, really." And for half a second, I thought Crystal DuLac was a mind reader like Morgan le Fey. Then I realized she was talking about the internship. "We'll send all the necessary details to your school in . . ." She opened the file and scanned my application. "Columbia, Missouri. Right?"

"Right."

"And they'll give you some kind of academic credit on your official transcript. The usual thing." Again, she peered over her glasses. "Any questions?"

"What exactly will I be doing here?"

"Oh, that," she said, ignoring her ringing cell phone. "All you have to do is follow my instructions, write a tidy little report on your activities here, and within six weeks, you'll know all there is to know about Malory Bede and White." She paused. "All, that is, that you *need* to know. Anything else?"

I shook my head. I mean, what could I say? Take me to the Grail. Or, who wears a Pendragon ring around here? Sure. But finally, I did ask, "Who will I be working for?"

"I'll supervise your work, of course. But, hmmm. Let me see." Ms. Dulac clicked a few keys on her sleek little laptop. "I think we'll assign you to BowWow Dog Chow and Cargill's Tummy Soothers. How does that sound?"

So I summoned up my courage. "Didn't you just land some new business with Dr. Gildas's Museum of Antiquities?"

"Ahhh. The Royal Regal account." Ms. DuLac broke into this huge smile. She had really beautiful teeth. "Auntie Nim has been coaching you, hasn't she?"

"We met at the Glastonbury dig."

"Of course! So you know all about this fascinating project!" She took off her glasses. "But alas, the Royal Regal account is off limits. Mr. Mordreaut works on that himself."

I wanted to shout, *Then why am I here?* Instead, I just gave her what must have been a lame little grin and got to my feet. "I better get going. It's a long bus ride back to Miss Nimuet's."

"So we'll see you tomorrow, then? There's a big meeting with BowWow Dog Chow."

"Sure," I mumbled. "Tomorrow's fine."

She walked me back to the elevator and shook my hand. I was tempted to stop off at every floor and look for the person with the Pendragon ring. But MBW was big. Really big—more than twenty floors, hundreds of people. So I decided to wait.

And two weeks slipped by.

Two long, miserable weeks. I went to a bunch of meetings for BowWow Dog Chow and Cargill's Tummy Soothers. I did lots of filing, answered the phones, and faxed reports to people all over Europe.

Erin was impressed. "It sounds like you have so much responsibility!" she e-mailed. "Think how that will look when you start applying to college next year."

But who cared? Because not once did I see anybody wearing a Pendragon ring. And not once did I get a glimpse of the Grail. In fact, nobody knew where it was for sure. The museum had closed "for repairs"; then Dr. Gildas fired Dr. Frazer.

"I told him what he wanted to hear: that the cauldron seems to be authentic," Dr. Frazer explained. "He doesn't want me around anymore."

Worst of all, I'd stopped dreaming about the Grail.

It was as if I'd never seen those Grail creatures, never heard them calling to me. And I didn't see any dancing sparkles either. All of that seemed like an old memory, something I'd just made up to fill those long afternoons at Maiden's Cottage.

But at night, I'd dream of the raven-haired boy. Dark, depressing dreams. Not nightmares really, though sometimes those dreams seemed realer than real, as if I didn't have a life.

As if I'd never been born.

Then I'd wake up, surprised to find myself lying in bed, listening to London outside my window. Surprised to find Mom looking young and happy, working every waking minute with Dr. Frazer on obscure King Arthur manuscripts they'd found in Dr. Nimuet's library.

Because Mom was in those dreams—but a different Mom somehow, one who never looked happy, a Mom I didn't know.

The phone must have rung at about six A.M. I was down in the kitchen because Merlin, who'd been missing for the past three days, had suddenly come home hungry. So I picked up the phone.

"There's been an . . . incident . . . at the museum."

It was Dr. Frazer, and before I could say anything, Mom gushed out a bunch of questions: "What kind of incident? How do you know? Are you working there again?"

"Archie called me this morning. Early," Dr. Frazer said slowly. "Asked me to consult on a special problem."

"What kind of problem?" Mom asked.

She must have picked up the phone in the library at exactly the same time I'd picked up in the kitchen because neither of them acted like they knew I was even there.

"It's hard to explain." Dr. Frazer's voice was almost shaking. "Impossible, really. But I don't think Felicity should work at MBW any longer."

Then the phone got so quiet I could hear Mom's breathing. Could she hear mine too? Who knows? If she did, she sure didn't let on. Because then Mom sighed, a really big sigh. "Does this have something to do with the Grail?"

Before Dr. Frazer could answer, Merlin jumped up on the counter and knocked over the sugar canister. It clattered to the floor and broke into about half a dozen chunks. Sugar whooshed across the floor like dry snow. I didn't say a thing. For a heartbeat, neither did Mom or Dr. Frazer. But just for a heartbeat . . .

"Are you on the line, Felicity?" Mom's voice sounded tired.

"Yeah."

Mom took another deep breath. "Good." Sometimes moms surprise you, don't they? I mean, they suddenly say or do the right thing. Well, this was one of those rare moments. "Now that we're both here, Ian, why don't you start from the top?" Mom was saying. "What's happened and why shouldn't Felicity work at MBW?"

But even with Mom on my side, things didn't turn out the way I thought, because instead of telling us the whole story, Dr. Frazer said, "I'm not at liberty to say. You'll have to trust me, Vanessa. Get Felicity out of there."

Then, all of a sudden, there was a lot of background noise—people yelling at one another, the wail of a siren. Someone even shouted, "Don't be an idiot, Frazer! No publicity!"

"I've got to go," he said. "Just trust me."

Then the line went dead.

Moments later, Mom shuffled into the kitchen and sank into one of the chairs. She didn't even notice the sugar all over the floor. She just leaned her elbows on the kitchen table and ran her hands through her hair. "I hate it when they say, 'trust me.'"

I knew exactly what she meant. Dad. "Trust me, Vanessa," he used to say before he went running across town to see . . . Well, you can guess.

Mom sat at the table so long, I had time to clean up the mess and dump it in the trash. Still, she didn't seem to notice.

Finally, she said, "Is something weird going on at MBW?" Merlin jumped up in her lap.

"I just work on dog food and Tummy Soothers," I said. "We might as well have stayed in Glastonbury."

Another long silence.

"I think I'll head over to the museum this morning," Mom said. "Maybe I can find out what's really going on."

"I'll nose around MBW. As usual."

Another even longer silence.

"Okay. But be careful." Then Mom's eyes met mine, and she looked tired and old—exactly the way she did in those dreams about the raven-haired boy.

Chapter 11

All in Black

And you shall know him by the ring on his finger,
a Traveler all in black.
—The Second Book of Nimue,
from the private collection of Vivian Nimuet

Mom left for the museum right away. But I had a little more time, time enough to think some more about that phone call. There was something in Dr. Frazer's voice I hadn't heard before—absolute panic. And fear.

There's been an incident. . . . Get Felicity out of there.

Then I remembered how he'd acted at Maiden's Cottage—you know, the night he tried to show Mom and me the Grail. He'd known something then, something secret, maybe even terrible. So before I left to catch the bus for MBW, I slipped Morgan le Fey's amber choker into my pack.

The necklace still scared me. Any time I came within ten feet of it, the thing lighted up, and if I touched it—well, it made my skin tingle. No way I was going to wear that choker around my neck. But on that fateful morning, I thought I might need a safety net. I was right about that. Wrong about the necklace . . .

Anyway, things were weird at MBW that morning, but not in a dangerous way. At least, not at first. Then right in the middle of a fax to BowWow Dog Chow, Crystal's assistant came running up, all breathless.

"Can you run a slide projector?" she asked.

I slid a copy of the fax into a big folder. "I do it all the time for Mom."

"Then come with me."

Well, I had a feeling about this one—one of *those* feelings. I could just sense something was going to happen. So when we rounded the corner by my work station, I grabbed the choker out of my pack and stuck it inside my official MBW internship notebook, which I had to take with me everywhere. Then we were in the elevator with Crystal, and she punched the button for the twenty-first floor. That's when I knew my intuition or whatever was right on target. Because the twenty-first floor—the entire twenty-first floor—was Mr. Mordreaut's private domain.

"Only *he* would plan an entire presentation around antiquated technology," Crystal was grumbling. "Can you imagine?"

"You mean Mr. Mordreaut's using a slide projector?"

Crystal adjusted her glasses. "Good heavens, no!" Her moon and star earrings jangled. "Everyone at MBW uses computers for these kinds of things. It's that disagreeable Dr. Gildas."

I started to tell her that I'd met Dr. Gildas before. Never in a million years would he want my help. But then never in a million years would I have ever wanted to help him—until now. So I kept quiet.

Crystal pressed a button on the control panel, and the elevator came to a smooth stop—somewhere between the nineteenth and twentieth floors. "Now about the projector," she said. "It's the remote or something. Won't work, and we don't even keep slide projectors around here anymore—much less spare parts."

"So Dr. Gildas will tell me when to advance the slides. Is that it?"

"Precisely." She adjusted the sleeves on her long, lacy blouse, then pressed another button, and the elevator started up again.

"Does Mr. Mordreaut approve of me being at this meeting?" I asked.

"Oh, he's not even here." She paused as the elevator doors opened, and we stared out at a gloomy dark hall, all black, except for a big red Pendragon carved into the opposite wall. "He's been delayed. Some kind of travel difficulties, I suppose."

But I barely heard her. That giant Pendragon . . . It gave me the creeps. Maybe Dr. Frazer was right. Maybe MBW was a pretty sinister place after all.

It seemed to me that the twenty-first floor was a labyrinth of darkness. Hallways curved and twisted, opening into windowless rooms. The lights were dim, dim, dim. Dozens of Pendragon chandeliers, carpeting like midnight. And everywhere there was the faint smell of that awful cologne or whatever. Not bad enough to make you sick really, but there—like a little buzzing headache that won't go away.

Crystal and her assistant didn't seem to notice. They just marched on straight ahead as if everything around us was as ordinary as, I don't know, a school cafeteria or something. I was just glad Mr. Mordreaut wasn't around—even glad that I'd stuffed that necklace in my notebook. What was it Morgan le Fey had said? *A magic crafted only for the wearer* . . .

Finally, we reached a kind of crossroads and directly ahead was this huge, gaping kind of room. Voices floated out of the doorway. We stepped inside and the voices stopped. Three men stared back at us—Dr. Gildas and two strangers dressed in expensive-looking suits.

"Meet Felicity Jones, Dr. Gildas," said Crystal, moving to the front of the room. "She'll run the projector for you this morning." She picked up a red phone and started to punch in a number. "Felicity, these are our clients from Royal Regal."

Before I could even shake their hands, Dr. Gildas was making a scene. "You expect me to work with this kid?" He started waving his arms around just like he'd done on the Tor, and muttering all kinds of nasty little insults about "today's youth." Not that he recognized me or anything. Dr. Gildas just refused to work with an intern on principle. Know what I mean?

"You either work with Felicity or you run the projector yourself," Crystal said finally.

Dr. Gildas glared at me. "Don't break anything."

I nodded and started checking out the projector. The lightbulb was screwed in tight, the forward and reverse buttons were right where I thought they'd be. The machine was just like the one Mom used back home; no matter what happened, Dr. Gildas couldn't blame me if his slide show flopped.

A couple of MBW people joined us. Then we started.

Dr. Gildas would bark out a command like, "Advance!" and I'd click the slide ahead. He'd wave his arms around at the front of the room, talk in a monotone, or stand right in front of the slide so nobody could see what we were supposed to be looking at. Then he'd shout, "Next slide." He never said please or thank you or anything like that.

This went on for about fifteen minutes— pictures of his museum mostly. Then we came to a whole series of slides at the Tor. Lots of close-ups of those string grids, a few shots of the Round Table security guards, even one or two of Dr. Frazer.

"And now, what you've been waiting for," Dr. Gildas announced. "Next slide, girl."

I advanced the tray. The next slide went into the slot, but there was nothing there. Except for a dark blue background, I mean.

"Next slide, girl!" he demanded.

I backed up the slide tray, took out that round plastic piece on top, fished out the slide, and held it up to the light.

"Maybe this was a test shot, sir."

Dr. Gildas trotted to the back of the room. "Impossible!" He snatched the slide from my hand, stared at it a moment, then tossed it aside. "Out of my way!" He pushed me against the back wall and went through about a dozen slides or so, all of the same empty dark blue background.

It was really an uncomfortable moment. You could just tell that those people from Royal Regal were not happy campers. I mean, why fly all the way from their headquarters in Kansas to look at a bunch of blue slides?

That's when Crystal stepped in. "Is there anything we can do, Dr. Gildas?"

He just scowled at her, as if it was *her* fault that the slides were empty. Then his eyes blinked and he turned toward me. "Did you say your name was Jones?"

I nodded.

"Jones as in daughter of Vanessa Jones?"

I nodded again.

This time, he really erupted—like one of those Pacific island volcanoes you see sometimes on public television. Crystal and her assistant struggled to get him out of the room. They were both crooning things like "It's not her fault," or "Really, my dear professor!" Finally, they got him into the hall.

Looking back on all this, it *was* pretty weird that those slides were nothing but background. At the time, given what I knew about Dr. Gildas, I just figured he'd probably screwed up the camera settings or something. Boy, was I wrong. We were all wrong. . . .

Anyway, Crystal came back and smoothed things over with the Royal Regal people. She had me clear away the projector and take a place at the conference room table. Then, in the darkness, she pressed a button up at the front of the room, and suddenly, these little computer screens popped right out of the table—one for every one of us.

At first, I was really tuned into the graphics on the screen, but Crystal's presentation went on and on. Or maybe it was the dark room. Or all those shifting colors on the screen. Anyway, I started to nod off. My eyes just wouldn't stay open. So I pulled out my internship notebook, made sure the necklace was safely tucked away in the front pocket, and started to doodle.

I drew a bunch of random lines up in one corner, then branched out across the top margin: a few daisies, three-dimensional boxes, a sketch of Crystal's moon and star earrings, her glasses. But then I really got into it, just let my pencil flow over the whole page. It was like a miracle or something, because I'm not an artist. Never have been. But you should have seen what I was drawing! These intricate, curvy lines. Creatures twined around and around one another. Ivy, oak, and laurel leaves. A woman standing in water.

Then, all of a sudden, I was sick. Sick with the smell of that cologne. The lights came up—bright, amazingly bright. I struggled to my feet, started to reach for my necklace, and came face to face with a man, all in black, a Pendragon ring on his finger.

"Felicity," I heard Crystal saying, "please meet Mr. Mordreaut."

But I pushed past the man in black, past a bunch of people standing in the doorway—including (I think) Dr. Frazer. I rushed down the hall, looking for a bathroom. I ran and ran and ran. Finally, I found one. A big, private bathroom—gold mirrors, red fixtures, black tile. It had to be Mr. Mordreaut's. But I didn't care.

I fell to my knees and puked my guts out.

And then, I swear this is true, when I was cleaning up, I looked down at my hands, my arms, my legs. I could see right through them. Like they weren't there. Like I wasn't there!

So maybe you can understand why I made two big mistakes—no, three. And here they are:

1. What I'd drawn back there in that conference room was a picture of the Grail.
2. I'd left both that picture and the amber necklace with my notebook.
3. All of that was back in the conference room—with Mr. Mordreaut.

Chapter 12

Second Sight

*Many people here believe in the notion of
Second Sight as surely as you and I believe in
gravity. They also say it passes from one
generation to another, usually through the
mother's side of the family.*
—Dr. Merlin Nimuet,
Folkways of the Somerset Country

Somehow, Crystal found me and took me back down to her office. Then I must have dozed off because when I really came to—without any more of that queasiness churning in my stomach—I was lying on the couch in her office, a cold compress on my head, a pile of Tummy Soother packages on the floor. Dr. Frazer was sitting across from me.

"Do you feel well enough for me to take you home now?" he asked.

"We've called your mum." Crystal leaned forward and her earrings jingled. "She wants you home right away."

I tried to sit up, but my arms and legs were so weak. I held up a hand to the light. At least it wasn't transparent. But Dr. Frazer and Crystal must have thought I was crazy or something because he said, "Perhaps we should send for a doctor, after all."

So I summoned up some energy. "What about the meeting?"

"Now that's more like it." Crystal smiled. "It's been postponed until tomorrow, and I think Mr. Mordreaut will assign you to the Royal Regal account."

I tried to smile. But to tell you the truth, if I never saw the insides of the twenty-first floor again in my life, it would have been too soon.

"He was very impressed with your work," Crystal went on.

"My work?"

She nodded.

Then it hit me. My drawing! "Where's my notebook?"

Crystal handed it to me, and I opened the flap. The drawing wasn't there—and neither was the necklace. It was almost enough to make me sick all over again.

"Let's get you out of here, Felicity," Dr. Frazer said suddenly. He helped me to my feet and took my pack from Crystal.

We were already in the elevator when Crystal called out, "Get well, sweetie! See you tomorrow!"

And just for a split second, a teeny tiny instant, there was something in her voice that reminded me of someone else. Then the elevator doors closed and we were gliding back down to the lobby.

Okay, you're right. I probably should have hit the button for the twenty-first floor and gone back for my things right then and there. But I still felt pretty shaky. I leaned against the back rail and shut my eyes.

"I thought I told you to stay away from here," Dr. Frazer began.

I was in no mood for a lecture; besides, it really wasn't any of his business, was it? So I said, "What are you doing here?"

"Archie phoned me about some trouble with the slides. He mentioned you were running the projector."

I opened my eyes. "Yeah. It was weird. All those slides were empty. Nothing but background." I waited for Dr. Frazer to explain. But he didn't. Instead he reached into his pocket and took out a piece of paper.

"Is this what you were looking for back in Ms. DuLac's office?"

I unfolded the paper and there it was—my sketch of the Grail.

"It caused quite a sensation," Dr. Frazer was saying. "Geoffrey Mordreaut, all the Royal Regal people."

The elevator stopped, the doors opened, and I just stood there. Staring. You can't believe how beautiful that drawing was. Absolutely perfect— like a da Vinci sketch or something—from the Renaissance.

Dr. Frazer led me into the lobby. "How do you explain this? The drawing, I mean." He paused. "Only a handful of people have seen the Grail— and I know them all. At least, I thought I did."

I looked out the window. What was I supposed to say?

"Felicity." Dr. Frazer nudged my arm. "I asked you a question."

He was being polite and everything, but I couldn't give him an answer. I just ran across the lobby and started to push through the revolving doors. And there he was again—the raven-haired boy, staring back at me as plain as day. His hand was on the opposite side of the glass, solid and real. I glanced down at mine—it had gone transparent again! I could see the push bar *through* my hand.

"You have the Second Sight, don't you, lass?" Dr. Frazer's voice was right behind me, but I ignored him, ignored everything except my see-through hand and Raven Head's laughter. Then I was out on the sidewalk, breathing in the grimy London air.

"There's a legend," Dr. Frazer was saying. "About Grail Keepers, the Maidens of Avalon." He turned and looked at me hard, really hard. Like he was seeing me for the very first time. "Until now, I never gave it much thought."

I backed away and looked at my hand, which was suddenly solid flesh again—my hand that had drawn such a beautiful, miraculous thing. Street sounds drowned out the boy's nasty laugh, but in my head, I heard Morgan le Fey.

Little Grail Keeper.

That's what she'd called me. Was that why I could draw the Grail? And if Dr. Frazer had made the connection, then what about Mr. Mordreaut?

Over Dr. Frazer's objections, I walked back to Miss Nimuet's flat. Alone. Somehow I needed the reality of walking, of putting one foot in front of the other, of feeling solid sidewalk under my feet.

Did I really want to go back to MBW? Did I really want to spend the rest of my internship hurling into a toilet? Because that's exactly where I'd be if I had to work alongside Mr. Mordreaut. No way that would put me any closer to the Grail. I stopped at a neighborhood park. Nobody was there, so I sat down in one of the swings and started moving back and forth. My arms and legs felt strong as I pumped higher and higher—perfectly solid, no blue sky showing through my veins. Maybe it was time to put all this Grail stuff behind me, to be real again. But when I got back to the apartment, Dr. Frazer pretty much made that impossible.

"Pack your bags tonight and head back to Glastonbury," he was saying. "I'll drive you back down."

Mom ignored him and wrapped an arm around my shoulder. "How are you feeling?"

"Okay," I said. "What's this all about? Why should we leave?"

Dr. Frazer took a deep breath. "Like I told you this morning. There's been an accident. All I can tell you now," he glanced over at Mom, "is that it was serious. And the Grail . . ." This time he looked right at me. "The Grail may have triggered it."

"Then the Grail's at the museum?" I asked.

Mom folded her arms. "I went to the museum today. It's reopened, business as usual. And except for you, Ian, nobody's talking about any accident—or the Grail."

"Can't you just trust me, Vanessa?" Dr. Frazer's face was exactly the same color as cold oatmeal. "I'm telling you all I can right now. Believe me." His voice sounded sad and desperate. Like he couldn't explain something—because it couldn't be explained. Which was something I could relate to.

Almost.

I mean, why wouldn't he just tell it straight? Unless . . .

Then it was like Mom was reading my mind because she said, "What kind of game are you playing? Has Gildas bought you off?"

We waited for an explanation. None came. Minutes just ticked away—and so did our friendship with Dr. Frazer.

After he'd gone, Mom stood with her back against the door. Finally, she said, "Why don't you lie down on the sofa? I'll bring you a pillow and afghan."

That's when I really knew how tired I was. And weak. So I let Mom baby me. She took my temperature (it was normal), then brewed some of her strong tea.

"Are you sure about the museum, Mom?" It wouldn't be the first time she'd jumped to conclusions.

"All the exhibits were open," she said.

"And the Grail? Did you see it? Is it there?"

Mom shook her head. "Who knows? If Gildas has the Grail and there was an accident, surely. . . ." Her voice trailed off. Then she asked, "Are you sure about MBW?"

Well, what could I say?

Mom didn't wait for an answer. "You don't have to go back," she said. "This Grail business really isn't your fight. Maybe it isn't mine either."

Your fate—and your mother's—are linked to the Grail.

I heard Morgan le Fey's voice as surely as I'd drawn that picture of the Grail, puked in Mr. Mordreaut's bathroom, seen the raven-haired boy. So I knew: The Grail was my fight. Our fight.

Then I turned my head toward the sofa and pretended to sleep.

Chapter 13

That Boy Is the Future

*Who can say with any certainty what powers
the Celts attributed to the Holy Grail? But it
seems that those who had the Grail in their
keeping may have believed they controlled the
human spirit.*
—Dr. Ian Frazer,
Archaeological Perspectives on the Ancient Celts

I stared into the back of that sofa for what seemed like an eternity, playing things over and over in my mind. Had Mom and I missed something? Could Dr. Frazer be telling the truth? Maybe if I concentrated hard enough, I could *See* the truth somehow. You know, any real danger at MBW or the accident at the museum. I cleared my mind and concentrated on the paisley blobs in the sofa material.

They blurred together exactly the way I imagined they should. But beyond that, nothing happened. No revelations. No great pronouncements. Nothing . . .

Until Morgan le Fey arrived.

"You foolish girl!"

I turned over, and there she stood in front of the sofa, shaking and pale, taking shape out of a pool of even paler sparkles. "How could you?"

"How could I what?"

"The necklace," she hissed. "How could you lose the necklace?"

"How could you expect me to wear it?" I fired back.

"It was made for you, you foolish girl. If you had worn it, no sickness would have touched you. And as for Mordred, he would not have detected you. Now he knows exactly who you are."

"Wait a minute," I said. "Who is Mordred?"

She glared at me. "Blind as a bat. Is that not the expression in your world?" Her words dripped poison. "Now you will have to retrieve the necklace from Mordred's lair."

Mordred.

That name again. Sure I'd heard it before— a name from Camelot. Like Bedivere, Lancelot, and Percival. Mordred was—and then I remembered. He was King Arthur's nephew . . .

And his son.

Morgan le Fey finished my thought.

So it was easy to make a connection to the Pendragon ring. "Mr. Mordreaut!" I gasped. "Mr. Mordreaut is Mordred!"

"Your mental powers are amazing," Morgan le Fey said flatly.

I sat up straight because it had all come back to me—all those stories Mom used to rattle off. "Mordred destroys Camelot. Kills or wounds the king. Isn't that right?"

The last of the sparkles were finally fading away, and so, almost, did Morgan le Fey. I could see the chair behind her—like she was a special effect in a movie. A glimmer, a ghost. Nothing more. I held my hand up to the light—and my hand was the same way! Transparent. Just like in Mr. Mordreaut's bathroom. Just like . . .

And then I saw the boy. He was sitting on the floor, dismembering a stuffed dragon. But the boy looked real. I mean, you couldn't see through him or anything.

"What's going on?" I demanded.

Morgan le Fey's eyes followed mine, and I knew she saw the boy. "Mordred, your Mr. Mordreaut, has seen the future, is living it now. But he knows how to change it as well."

It was like being trapped in a bad sci-fi movie, one about a parallel universe or something. But *this* was happening right before my eyes, and I didn't have the script.

Raven Head got up and walked over to Dr. Nimuet's desk. He opened the center drawer and took out a pair of scissors. He snipped them open and shut, smiling a wicked little smile. Then, clutching the scissors, he shoved open the French doors and dashed down the hall.

Who is this boy? my inner voice cried. *Why is he taking over my life?*

"Use your Sight, Felicity." Morgan le Fey leaned closer. "Did I not tell you that the Grail had been stolen from my time? Think, think about what that has to mean!"

I shook my head and stared down at my hands. My see-through hands.

"And it has been taken from yours, has it not?" she persisted.

"So?"

"So, the Grail is missing in the past. It is missing in the here and now. Unless you find it in the not-too-distant future, you, like me and most of the others in Camelot, will cease to exist."

Cease to exist.

Did she mean I was slowly fading away, fading into nothingness? Was this my fate? I looked down at my hands again. Through them, I could see the outline of the paisley on the sofa, even the seams in the cushions. But I could also feel the blood racing through my veins, see the rise and fall of my chest. Never in my whole life had I been so conscious of living, of breathing in and out. Could the raven-haired boy feel this way, too?

Morgan le Fey pointed to the hall. "In a world without the Grail, that boy is the future. With each passing day, the possibility of his existence grows stronger, just as mine—and yours—grow weaker."

And then I had another flash. *Is Mom fading too? Is this the fate we share?*

Morgan le Fey glanced around the room. Then she walked over to Dr. Nimuet's desk. At first, I couldn't see what she'd picked up, but when she turned back toward me, she was holding what looked like a crystal paperweight. As she got closer, I could tell this wasn't any ordinary paperweight. I mean, inside it were dozens and dozens of amber and purple sparkles—glittering, dancing, and whirling around like lightning bugs.

"This will show you what may come to pass," she said, holding the crystal at about eye level.

"Study it well. Open your mind and spirit to the lights."

Then those sparkles just took over. Shimmering and spinning like pixie dust. Only this was real magic. How had it come into Dr. Nimuet's hands, I remember wondering.

And then I was inside the crystal, and those amber and purple lights were brushing ever so softly against my skin—little prickles that gave me goose bumps. And the whole world was first purple, then gold, then purple again. The colors swam around me, then brightened in a sudden burst.

I stood alone in Dr. Nimuet's library.

Or was it?

Sure, all the bookshelves were there. So was his desk. But everything was different somehow. The room was darker, the air heavier. A thick black carpet stretched across the floor. The walls were painted bloodred. I scanned the titles of the books on one massive shelf—they were about economics, politics, business. Not a single history or collection of medieval romances among them—nothing about the age of Arthur. All of Dr. Nimuet's rare and valuable books were gone! Just as I moved to another shelf, the French doors slammed open and the boy was back. He was laughing again, that nasty little laugh that made my skin crawl. He tossed the scissors and a handful of red hair on the sofa. That's when Mom ran into the room.

Mom!

She looked frazzled, pale, tired—the way I'd seen her in all those nightmares. But her hair was ragged, cut so close to the scalp she was almost bald. Blood trickled down her neck.

"Look what you've done!" she cried.

The boy just laughed.

She reached for him; he slipped away, quicker than a shadow.

"I'll tell your father." But Mom's voice sounded weak, tentative.

"Papa won't care," the boy said.

Mom's face kind of crumpled, and I could tell she knew it was true.

"It's your fault anyway," he continued. "I told you I wanted to see the alligators today. You should have taken me to the zoo." He picked up the scissors and snipped the air. "See what taking a nap gets you!"

Blood from the cuts on her scalp gathered in a little pool at the base of her throat.

Then I heard the front door open, and the boy cried out, "Papa!" He ran toward the French doors, and suddenly the whole room was enveloped by that sickening smell.

Geoffrey Mordreaut!

He whisked the boy into his arms and glanced over at Mom. "You've had your hair done." His voice was mean. "Have you hurt yourself too?"

Mom started to say something, but suddenly Mr. Mordreaut whirled toward my direction. Then he started walking right toward me. "Who's there?" he shouted.

Somehow, I knew to summon the sparkles. They came swirling around, hiding me, sheltering me. My skin tingled against all that energy, and then I was swept away in a flood of light. Back to Dr. Nimuet's library—the one I knew, where Morgan le Fey was waiting.

Chapter 14

Daughters of Avalon

She was never to forget that first sight of Avalon. . . .
Women, robed in dark-dyed dresses . . . came down the path
toward them. . . .
—Marion Zimmer Bradley, *The Mists of Avalon*

Morgan le Fey sat small and still in the high-backed chair in Dr. Nimuet's library. "So now you *See*," she said.

I *Saw* far too well, just like in that lawyer's office—Mom, Dad, the divorce. But this was worse. Way worse. "Mordred will marry Mom," I said slowly. "And I will never be born."

"Precisely." Her voice was sharp and hard. "But only if you are unable to thwart his plans."

"What do you mean?"

At first, Morgan le Fey didn't answer. She stood there, dark and silent like those standing stones at Stonehenge. Across the hall, I could hear Mom banging around in the kitchen, making sandwiches or something for supper. Then Morgan le Fey took a deep breath and her voice came out in a whispery kind of echo. "You are the Maiden in the here and now," she said, "who transports the Grail."

I took a deep breath. "The Grail Keeper legend?"

It was that time between day and night when everything goes gray—the trees and sky outside, the room around you. You know, that almost magical moment when it's neither day or night, when everything is just . . . waiting. So it was hard to see Morgan le Fey's face, and she was guarding her thoughts.

I decided to put the question another way. "Why would Mordred bother with Mom?" I asked. "Or with me?"

Finally, Morgan le Fey answered. "You are both daughters of Avalon, the last ones known to us in these perilous days." She walked to the library window, and I followed her. We stared down at the gray, gray street below. A car honked, angry voices shot up from the sidewalk, a distant siren wailed. How could Mom and I be daughters of a place that didn't exist?

Your world has the most curious concept of reality—a thought Morgan le Fey let me hear, full of sadness and disappointment. There was more:

It has been your mother's undoing. Will it be yours also?

What was I supposed to make of that? So I said, "Why don't you ever give me a straight answer?"

Morgan le Fey turned. "There is no straight answer. That is another of your illusions."

"How about the truth? Is that an illusion too?" And for just a second, Morgan le Fey reminded me of Dad, just before he walked out on Mom and me. The way he never answered our questions, the way he tried to gloss things over or make them way more complicated than they needed to be.

And then the theater lights across the street blinked on, and it was like Morgan le Fey had walked onto a stage. Her red hair, braided and twisted across the top of her head; the long, flowing gown; the Grail creatures embroidered across her cape. Even pale and tired, she was beautiful. Magical. Dad had never been that.

She touched my hair—softly, the way Mom always does, and then she said, "Did you not once observe that except for my garments and jewels, I could pass as a member of your mother's family?"

It seemed like ages ago, but sure, I'd thought that.

"That is because we are one family." She paused. "Or perhaps I should say that you and your mother are part of *my* family. A family of women. Grail Keepers. Trained on the Isle of Avalon until the dawn of the last century, when all of this"—she motioned toward the London street—"extinguished our learning. Is that enough truth for you?"

"It's a start," I said.

"Your mother has fought her lineage harder than you, refusing to acknowledge even the Sight. The academic interest she nurtures in Arthurian 'legend' . . . It is all that is left of her gifts."

"Maybe not," I said. "I think she sees those time sparkles. At least sometimes."

Morgan le Fey smiled. "Is that so?" She stroked the side of my cheek. "Perhaps our magic is stronger than even I thought possible. For you, little one, saw the Shimmers of Time almost from the beginning." She lightly touched my shoulders. "You are our last hope."

So I thought the inevitable question.

Why am I your last hope?

Can you not See *the answer?* Morgan le Fey's mind flashed back.

I walked over to Dr. Nimuet's desk and picked up that paperweight again. The minute I touched it, the sparkles inside started dancing, swirling into all those wonderfully familiar shapes—the Grail creatures. They were back, and I could hear their voices again! Okay, okay, so I couldn't really understand them. But those creatures were talking to me. *Talking*—after such a long silence.

And then I *knew*.

I was the last hope because the Grail had chosen me. I was the Grail Keeper it wanted in the here and now. It spoke directly to me! For a second, I felt unafraid. Just half a second . . .

Because Morgan le Fey was saying something about Mordred and his mother, who was some kind of renegade Grail Keeper. "She bequeathed her share in the Shimmers of Time to him before her death. Now he has mastered Time travel so well that he can detect the presence of another traveler, even in a vision. He is a deadly adversary."

A deadly adversary.

That didn't surprise me. Not one bit. So I said, "He saw me. In that last vision. The one with his, with their . . . " Then I couldn't go on. That awful picture of Mom and Mordred and . . .

"Their son." Morgan le Fey said it easily, fearlessly. "In a way, Mordred has recreated his own beginning, choosing a kinswoman, albeit a distant one, to give birth to his heir. A son that will live on in a future that Mordred has created for himself. For everyone."

"Mordred will succeed in your world, too, won't he?"

"It is possible," she said softly. "By stealing the Grail in our Time, and destroying it in yours, Mordred could ensure that the quest for the Grail will never transpire. All those knights who should pursue the Grail will simply grow old. Their tales will never be told. King Arthur's court will pass into oblivion."

"But this hasn't happened yet," I said, with a sudden *knowing*. "There's still time to stop him." By now, the room was completely dark, except for the flashing lights from the theater across the street.

"Mordred must absolutely and forever destroy the Grail for his future to unfold," Morgan le Fey said slowly. "He has not yet taken that final step."

"Is that where this business with MBW fits?"

Morgan le Fey nodded. "For a brief sliver of Time, before the worlds shift, Mordred can accumulate a vast fortune from Royal Regal and with it, establish a financial empire."

"That's why he hasn't destroyed the Grail."

"True," she said. "But know this, Felicity. He who controls the Grail, controls the human spirit. Already our worlds are suffering. The joy, the life, the magic of things fanciful and creative are leeching away." Morgan le Fey walked to the window and watched the theater lights across the street flash red, green, yellow, white. "In my time, bards have put aside their harps, potters have abandoned their wheels. In yours, song, dance, art, and story will pass away." She motioned toward the street. "That very theater closes tonight."

Which reminded me, for some strange reason, of the empty playground on the way back from MBW. Empty, on a perfectly beautiful afternoon. Would this be part of Mordred's future too? A world where even little kids wouldn't remember how to play? Would they all turn out like Raven Head?

Morgan le Fey sighed. "Who can say with any certainty what will come to pass if Mordred controls the Grail's destiny? My Sight will not show me the full extent of that future, perhaps because I cannot see beyond the life of the last Grail Keeper."

And if Mordred succeeds, that would be Mom. He or the boy will destroy her.

The paperweight grew heavy and cold in my hands. The purple and amber lights swirled into darkness, drawing me in, into a vast nothingness, an expanse of deep and silent cold.

Mordred's world. Mordred's future.

I called out for Mom. I called out for anyone. But this world was so silent and so very cold. So still. Like a body in a coffin. Like a corpse.

Morgan le Fey must have touched my hand or something because the cold and darkness lifted, the sparkles returned, and I could hear Mom making cooking noises in the kitchen.

"Do not look too far into the future," Morgan le Fey said, taking the paperweight from my hand, "for there lies despair. Concentrate on the here and now."

Then Mom called out, "Felicity! Can you eat some supper?"

"In a minute," I called back, feeling suddenly hungry and homesick. Homesick for Mom and Merlin and all the things we always did in an ordinary day.

That broke the spell.

Morgan le Fey moved across the library and repeated her order. "Concentrate on the here and now." Then she held out another one of those little clay jars.

"You will need this, of course."

"You know how I feel about that stuff," I said, turning away.

"You prefer to return to Mordred's lair with your stomach on fire?"

"Why would I want to go back?" I got to my feet slowly.

"For the necklace. Without it, you are vulnerable to his magic." Morgan le Fey raised her arms, and the sparkles swirled around the hem of her gown, then higher, and higher still, until the jar itself was enveloped in purple and amber light.

I stared at that jar. It just hung there, suspended in color like one of Morgan le Fey's jewels. I hated the thought of drinking that stuff, but I hated the sickness it prevented even more. Because I knew she was right. I had to go back— to the twenty-first floor. So I reached through the sparkles and took the jar.

Chapter 15

Something Passed Between Us

Through the might of Morgan le Faye . . .
By subtleties of science and sorcerers' arts . . .
—Sir Gawain and the Green Knight

I stopped the MBW elevator on the twentieth floor and stared down at that vial of stomach potion. How fast would it work? How much should I take? This stuff didn't come with instructions from the drugstore. My mouth went all dry and my stomach felt jittery. But what choice did I have?

It was still early, not yet seven A.M., and the only person I'd seen so far was a janitor. My MBW ID, which worked like an electronic passkey, had gotten me into the building. As for a plan, I really didn't have one—except to get in and out of Mordred's place. Fast.

Actually, what I thought might be a plan hadn't worked. Already. The night before, Mom and I had eaten mac and cheese together, then watched an old movie. Finally, after she went to bed, I slipped back into Dr. Nimuet's library and tried using his paperweight again—to *See* where Mr. Mordreaut would be when I broke into the twenty-first floor. When that didn't work, I even tried to check out Dr. Frazer's story about the accident at the museum.

It's not that the paperweight didn't show me anything. The dancing sparkles sucked me back into the crystal all right, just like before. But I had no control over what I *Saw*. First, there was an old, old man in long flowing robes; he was walking through an apple orchard with a beautiful girl. Next, I saw a much younger Mr. Mordreaut—Mordred, really—watching a woman, maybe his mother, gather a cluster of Time sparkles into a silver cauldron. Finally, the scene skipped way ahead in time, almost into the present—Miss Nimuet with a sprightly old man, Dr. Nimuet probably. In between each scene, I saw nothing but sparkles and the whole experience was like watching TV with the mute button switched on. I couldn't hear anything except a faint whooshing sound. Then I just gave up. Obviously, Morgan le Fey must have guided me into the vision I'd seen of Mom, Mordred, and their son.

So there I was. Stalled on the twentieth floor, staring down at that little clay vial. I pressed my back against the wall and closed my eyes. The paperweight, which I'd thrown into my pack in a moment of desperation, jammed against my spine. My so-called magic seemed pretty powerless, especially if Morgan le Fey either had to coach me from the sidelines or drug me to make it work.

Then, all of a sudden, I *Saw* the Grail.

Glorious, bright, perfect. Bursts of amber and purple lights swirled all around, illuminating first one creature, then another. And for the first time, I could hear each individual voice of each individual creature. One was soft and low. Another deep and fierce. With a whole range of harmonies in between. Over them all was the voice of their goddess. She gave me courage.

So I took the stopper out of the vial and drank it dry. The potion slid down my throat like those cherry cokes I used to drink with Dad. Fizzy, sweet, and kind of thick. Then I pressed a button and the elevator started to move again—upward, toward the twenty-first floor.

*   *   *

It was even darker than I remembered. Those red dragon lights shone no brighter than flickering candles, and the hallway curved into blackness in both directions. I stepped onto the thick, heavy carpet and took a deep breath. The air smelled a little damp and stale, like a big hotel. But otherwise it was clear. No aftershave. No nausea.

Maybe even no Mordred . . .

Okay, so I *knew* the potion had just neutralized that smell, but there are times when you have to think positive or you'd never dare to do what you have to do. So in that logical, rational part of my brain—the side I could pretty much control—I decided that Mordred was back in Morgan le Fey's Time, or even somewhere in that future he was trying to create for himself. I decided he definitely wasn't anywhere on the twenty-first floor.

Once I made that decision, then the next one was easy. Obviously, I had to head back toward that private bathroom where I'd thrown up because maybe, just maybe that bathroom was part of an apartment or something—what Morgan le Fey called Mordred's lair. Wouldn't that be the logical spot to hide my necklace?

So I turned sharp to the right and charged into the darkness. Decisive action, my dad used to say, was the only way to drive away fear. But I couldn't charge ahead forever. I mean, the darkness, the curving walls, the closed doors—they forced me to slow down, to take measured steps, to open every door. Slowly, silently.

Most of the rooms that were unlocked were dark, cavelike places—conference rooms. Some big, some small. But in every one there was a wicked overhead light—more Pendragons—that flickered over a square slab of a table. Now you're probably asking, were any of these rooms THE conference room, the one where Mordred had swiped the necklace in the first place?

Honestly, I couldn't say. The bigger rooms all looked alike. But I searched every single one, large and small. I found absolutely nothing. I even searched a supply closet. But it just had the usual things: MBW stationery and envelopes, boxes of pens and pencils, and stacks of computer supplies. Finally, I decided to retrace my steps.

I passed the elevator, started down the opposite hall, and stopped at the first curve. The air smelled kind of like flowers—fresh, pleasant-smelling flowers. It occurred to me suddenly that

Mordred's private bathroom had a bouquet of white lilies in a black and red vase. So I was probably close, and the rational side of my brain kicked in again. I could either:

1. Head back to the elevator and call the whole thing off.

Or:

2. Give the crystal paperweight another try.

But then I decided if it somehow managed to show me what I needed to *See,* Mordred would probably know about it. He'd *See* me as clearly as I *Saw* him. That's when I realized I had a third option.

So I took a deep breath (it really does help), closed my eyes, and summoned up a vision of the Grail. Every last Grail creature was there—perfect, clearly etched in gold. Bursts of amber and purple lights exploded above the cauldron, then fell back into its depths. But they lighted my way down that last hall, and I found what I was looking for.

The apartment, I mean.

Its open doorway was straight ahead. I passed the bathroom on the left, and there were the lilies, a big full bunch of them. The living room or whatever was around the corner. And you guessed it—everything was black and red. The sofa, the chairs, the coffee table, the expensive-looking computer equipment. Talk about a color fixation. Anyway, I stood there, glued to the spot, for a long time. Waiting, listening. When nothing happened, I moved fast. Really fast. Pulling open drawers, looking under furniture, checking every cubbyhole in that ebony desk. Then I noticed the dining room.

The table was set for breakfast—a breakfast for two. In the center of the table was a big, black lacquered box. A logical place for a necklace, right? So it didn't take long to cross the living room, jump up a couple of stairs, and pop open that box. It wasn't even locked.

But it was empty, except for a pair of cuff links.

"Is this what you're looking for?"

Mr. Mordreaut. Mordred.

And he just stood there smiling—this dazzling, white, beautiful smile—holding out my necklace in his hand. Then he dropped it into the pocket of his black kimono, so smooth and silky that it slid across his bare chest. His bare, muscled chest.

Okay, I promise I'm not writing a sleazy grocery-store romance or anything, but you can't believe how incredibly good-looking he was. Not that tall really, or broad-shouldered. But Mordred had this lean, dark—well, sexy look about him. No wonder Mom was going to fall for him in an alternate universe.

So I'm standing there, with my tongue practically hanging out, and he says, "Won't you stay for breakfast and tell me how such a valuable necklace came into your possession?"

Before I could say anything, he touched my arm—softly. You'd expect a cold, snaky touch, right?

Wrong. Way wrong.

It was like a spark or a surge of energy or something passed between us—a connection. Talk about magic! Or maybe just plain old chemistry. So of course, I said yes.

We sat down and his arm brushed against mine as he poured me a big glass of orange juice. "I assume you're feeling well enough to eat?" he asked.

I nodded and reached for my juice.

He poured a cup of coffee, then added lots of cream.

"That's how I like to drink it," I said.

"What a surprising coincidence." He flashed that beautiful smile of his, passed me the coffee, then poured himself another cup. "Now," he said, "what's that old crone been telling you about me?"

"Old crone?" Was he talking about Miss Nimuet?

"You know," he replied. "Morgan le Fey."

Before I could say anything, Mordred smiled. "Don't be sucked into the glamorous aura she creates for herself. Surely you're bright enough to see through it." Then he started quoting this poem about an old hag who set out to trick Sir Gawain. One of the passages went something like this:

Her body was stump and squat
Her buttocks bulging and wide. . . .

"That's not the Morgan le Fey I know," I said.

Mordred smiled again. "She wears many faces, assumes many shapes." He quoted more lines from the poem—about how crafty she was, how dishonest.

"I hope I haven't confused you. But these old poems and legends have their own kind of truth, don't you think?" He shoved a plate of pastries in my direction. "But you haven't eaten anything. Here. The scones are good. The chocolate croissants are better."

They did look fabulous. Fat, flaky croissants just bursting with chocolate.

But the minute that chocolate hit my mouth, I was sick again. Sick with the revolting smell of aftershave—so sweet it was foul. But I couldn't, wouldn't be sick in front of him. So I set the croissant aside and tried willing the nausea away. That didn't work. Neither did the juice that I drank ever so slowly, or the deep breaths I took while Mordred munched on a raspberry scone. Uggg. I bit my lip and wrapped my hands around the edges of my chair. How had this happened? Had Morgan le Fey's potion run out of gas?

Then the phone rang, and Mordred cursed. He reached into his pocket and took out a sleek cell phone. And for an instant, I saw it—my necklace! The amber stones all golden and bright in the folds of his black silk. Somehow, just seeing them there took the edge off my urge to puke.

"I told you not to call me here this morning!" Mordred barked, turning away from me. "He's what?" The opening in his pocket widened. "Crystal, you fool!"

I could make out the sound of her voice through the phone. She was talking fast, not giving Mordred a chance to interrupt. Her voice was soothing somehow, calming, like the sight of my necklace in Mordred's pocket. It didn't make the sickness go away exactly, but it cleared my head. And Morgan le Fey's words came back to me.

You would not have felt any sickness if . . .

So I reached, reached, reached.

Mordred shifted his weight, and the pocket slipped out of my grasp.

"I won't see him now!" Mordred shouted. "Fetch him back down yourself."

More talk from Crystal—enough for me to reach the pocket. My hand slipped inside. I felt the warmth of Mordred's skin through the silk. Then I felt something else: the warmth, the strength of Morgan le Fey's magic.

The necklace was in my hand.

I pulled it out of Mordred's pocket and dashed for the hall. It was like I was seeing everything for the first time. Not just the tiles in the bathroom or the lilies or the Pendragon lights. Everything! From those chocolate croissants to the muscles on Mordred's chest. A frantic, fast little flashback—but this time, I saw, *Saw* through his magic, his charm.

Charm!

Mordred had bewitched me for sure, or else there had been some flaw in me—or my magic—that had almost, almost made me believe in him.

I tried to run faster, but the sickness was still with me, slowing me down, making me dizzy. And Mordred was right behind me. I could feel his breath on the back of my neck.

"You little witch," he hissed.

That must have cleared my head completely, because I knew exactly what to do. I slipped the necklace around my throat. It felt warm against my skin, comforting, soothing.

A magic crafted only for the wearer.

But my necklace didn't feel magical, exactly. It felt perfect—as perfect as the shape of the Grail. And in that instant, the sickness passed. Mordred backed off and I raced to the elevator.

Chapter 16

To The Center of Nothing

The quest for enlightenment begins.
—TV commercial, MBW for Royal Regal

I crashed right into an old man with thinning white hair who was getting off the elevator. He took one look at me and said, "You're the very person I wanted to see today!" He latched on to my arm.

"But I was just leaving, sir," I said, trying to pull away. I swear I'd never seen him before in my life.

"Nonsense!" His grip tightened and the elevator doors closed before I could break free.

"You're here early, Harold." It was Mordred, his face as hard as those marble tables in the conference rooms. He was holding a wicked-looking letter opener—long and narrow with a jagged edge and a bloodred handle.

He was holding it like a knife.

Our eyes met—Mordred's and mine. Then he grinned at me—exactly like the raven-haired boy—and slipped the letter opener back into his pocket.

"Have you two been properly introduced?" Mordred's voice was as smooth as that silk kimono of his. "Felicity Jones. Harold Bingley, chief executive officer at Royal Regal, our most valuable client."

"No need to brownnose, Geoff." Mr. Bingley turned down the hall as if he knew exactly where he was going. "I'm here to talk about this young lady," he said. "After seeing that Grail drawing of hers yesterday, I want her in today's meeting."

Mordred's eyes burned into my necklace. I could feel the amber and silver turning warm around my neck. Not hot, just warm—like its magic, my magic, was hard at work. Then Mordred's eyes kind of flashed, the choker cooled down, and he said, "Sure. Why not?"

Better the enemy you know. . .

It was Mordred's voice I heard, inside my head. He flashed me another one of those smiles and sent me the rest of his thought. *Now that we understand each other, Grail Keeper.*

I tried to hide my thoughts, to keep them deep down inside. But I knew he knew: I was scared. Scared to death—and not because of that letter opener. I mean, think about it. His mind was talking to mine, exactly the way Morgan le Fey's did. And if he could read my mind, then there was no way I could save the Grail—or Mom or even myself—from him.

Noble ambitions. Mordred's thought again.

The elevator opened and Crystal got out.

"Is everything okay?" she asked, putting her hands on my shoulders. Her jewelry jingled, just like it always did, and somehow, suddenly, everything was okay. It was like, I don't know, a wall or curtain or something had just closed down all around me. Mordred couldn't pick at my brain—and I couldn't hear into his, which was fine. Believe me.

He went back to his apartment, and I followed Crystal and Mr. Bingley into one of the big conference rooms. Now maybe you're wondering why I didn't run to the nearest exit and just go home. After all, I had the necklace. That's why I broke into Mordred's in the first place, right?

Right.

But despite everything—the way Mordred had read my mind, even that wicked letter opener—I was starting to feel an obligation to see things through. Maybe it was the magic in all that amber around my neck. Maybe it was the memory of the Grail voices. Or maybe it was the blood snaking down Mom's neck. But I was a Grail Keeper, wasn't I? The Grail had chosen me. So I sat down next to Crystal and whispered, "What's this meeting about anyway?"

It wasn't long before the conference room started filling up—MBW people, Mordred, Dr. Gildas, even Dr. Frazer. He slipped into a chair next to mine.

"You shouldn't be here," he said.

I didn't bother to answer.

The room went dark except for a single spotlight shining down on a black box at one end of the table. Behind it stood Mr. Bingley's assistant, a guy in a suit named Gary Sands.

"After intensive research into polymers, colors, and consumer trends . . ." Mr. Sands took a step back and snapped open the black box. "I give you the Royal Regal Infant Grail!"

Everybody gasped.

Because there on its black velvet stand was a stubby, kind of squashed-down covered bowl with a spout sticking out of the top. And instead of the Grail creatures, there were these teddy bears and bunny rabbits joined together like paper dolls, dancing around its sides.

So I breathed a huge sigh of relief.

Well, think about it. If the baby Grails were that ugly, they'd never sell, and at least part of Mordred's plan would collapse like a house of cards.

The lights came back up and Mr. Sands started talking again, really fast like he was trying to explain why the thing was so hideous.

"Sit down, Gary." Mr. Bingley interrupted. "It's garbage. That thing will never sell."

"You're right it won't sell!" shouted Dr. Gildas. "You can't possibly meet your financial obligations to my museum with that worthless hunk of plastic."

"But we convinced you, didn't we?" Mr. Bingley said slowly. "We can't design even a baby Grail until we see the real one." Then he looked straight at me. "That girl there apparently knows more about the Grail than we do. We all saw her drawing, before she was shuttled out of here like a top-secret weapon."

Then everybody was staring at me, and I couldn't think of a thing to say. How could I explain? Why would I want to?

Mordred moved to the front of the room. "He has a point, Archie. You and Frazer here haven't even provided the good people at Royal Regal with snapshots of your grand relic. How can you expect them to reproduce something they haven't seen?"

A shiver went up my spine, a long, cold, rippling shiver. Those blank blue slides the day before. . . and Dr. Frazer's reluctance to explain them.

"Why don't you bring us the Grail, Archie?" Mordred said smoothly. "You've kept it under lock and key long enough. Bring it here. This afternoon."

Right. So you can annihilate it.

The thought came screaming through my head, maybe even passed into Mordred's. He looked at me and smiled.

Then Crystal spoke up. "No need to rush into anything. Besides, ladies and gentlemen, we have an advertising campaign to review."

*   *   *

Then the conference room went really, really, *really* dark. For an instant, I thought I was back in Dr. Nimuet's crystal again, trapped in that black, cold, hopeless void I'd *Seen* with Morgan le Fey. But once the sound system kicked in, I knew where I was, although I couldn't shake this feeling of total despair. Medieval sounding music poured into the room, and all those little computer screens around the table popped up. Every screen showed the same image: the MBW Pendragon against a black background.

But from that point on, I lost track of everything—except the computer screen in front of me and the images that shot across it.

The Pendragon dissolved slowly, like burning embers, and the screen went black. In the distance, I heard a low, chilling moan that rose to a chorus—the Grail creatures. Black faded to gray, then whirled itself into a churning fog. I stumbled over a rocky hilltop littered with ugly yellow stones shaped like tiny Grails. They crunched and shattered underfoot.

Broken dreams, my inner voice whispered. *Millions of broken dreams.*

When I reached the top, the fog lifted and a valley full of shattered Grail stones stretched all the way to the horizon. But somehow the cries of the wounded Grail creatures grew closer, more urgent. Where were they? What was happening to them?

Mordred laughed, or at least I think he did. And his laughter sent me across the valley to the next peak, and I found myself staring into a great abyss of unbearable cold. My whole body started to shake and my hands went numb. I watched as amber and purple sparkles shot out of the abyss, then dissolved into black, robbed of their color and brightness.

Extinguished forever. Mordred's voice and more laughter.

And this time, I fell. Into the abyss.

I fell and fell and fell, through those dying amber and purple lights. Down, down, to the center of Time. To the center of Nothing. And there was Mordred. He and his son together, tending a terrific fire that burned black, cold, silent. It enveloped the Grail completely.

The creatures were past crying, past moaning even. The cauldron itself a mass of melting gold—burning, dying in that silent, black fire. For an instant, I saw the goddess at the cauldron's center, then she was eaten by the flames.

Do not look too far into the future for there lies despair.

Morgan le Fey's voice. Or was it?

Concentrate on the here and now.

Her words, but not her voice. A jolt of reality. I stopped shaking, suddenly aware of where I was. In the conference room. At MBW.

"You call this advertising?" Mr. Bingley growled, as the lights flickered back on. "A sorceress who sours babies' milk? A good fairy in combat boots?"

Is that what everybody else had seen? I touched one of the amber stones on my necklace and *knew* beyond a shadow of a doubt. The great black fire, the moaning Grail creatures. . . . Only my screen had run that program.

I glanced at Mordred, expecting him to send me one of his unsettling, knowing thoughts. But his attention was focused entirely on Mr. Bingley. Maybe Mordred didn't know what I'd seen.

Then, out of nowhere, I heard them calling to me—the Grail creatures. All their voices in a happy chorus of sound. I can't tell you how glad I was to hear them again! To know that they were alive and well and still in need of me.

"Those commercials are a disaster," Mr. Bingley was saying. "Your intern there could do better work."

Crystal's jewelry jingled again. "You know, Geoff," she said, "That's not a bad idea. Perhaps we should give Felicity a shot at this campaign."

Mordred's voice came back low and sinister. "If you think it matters. After all, creativity is nothing without a good product."

Mr. Bingley nodded. "I get your drift, Geoff." He turned to Dr. Gildas. "The girl needs to see the Grail before she does any creative work."

"You can't put Felicity at risk!" Dr. Frazer was on his feet. "Not after what happened yesterday."

Dr. Gildas cut him off. "Risk? What risk?" He leaned back in his chair and rested his hands on his stomach. "If MBW and Royal Regal need to see the Grail to produce profitable work, then we should do everything in our power to accommodate them."

Everybody started talking all at once—everybody, that is, except Dr. Frazer and me. You could just tell where this meeting was going. Gildas would drive over to MBW with the Grail and Mordred would burn it into oblivion.

So I pushed back my chair and stood up. The Grail creatures' voices in my head grew louder, stronger, sharper. I cleared my throat. "I don't need to see the Grail to come up with a new campaign. I mean, I have this to inspire me." I waved my Grail drawing in the air. "Just give me until Friday, Mr. Bingley. You'll like my work. I promise."

Did Mordred hear the desperation in my voice? Probably. Probably everybody did. Finally, Mr. Bingley took out a handkerchief and wiped his forehead. "Okay. Okay. Go ahead and work something up, little lady. But I don't want to look at another campaign until I see the Grail myself. In living color." He nodded at Dr. Gildas. "Bring me the Grail on Friday and I'll bring you a nice, fat check to sweeten the deal."

Dr. Gildas's eyes lit up.

"I'll make you the same offer, Geoff." Mr. Bingley grinned. "You'll get the balance of your creative fee day after tomorrow. We'll look at Felicity's work and the Grail then."

Mordred eased around the conference table and stopped right behind me. My choker flashed hot against my skin. His arm rested on my shoulder. "Thanks for the set-up, Grail Keeper," Mordred whispered. Then he left the conference room. Everybody else left too. Except Dr. Frazer and me.

He just sat there, staring down at his hands. "They don't know what they're dealing with, Felicity. Believe me."

Chapter 17

Far More Dangerous

The ancient texts indicate a belief that those who look upon the Grail without clarity of vision shall go mad or die. The phrase is an odd one: clarity of vision. Surely this implies more than purity of heart. An inner knowing perhaps? The foundation for those old wives' tales about Second Sight?
—Dr. Vanessa Jones,
Exploring the Myth of the Grail Keeper

Dr. Frazer and I sat in the dark, empty conference room under that flickering Pendragon light for a long time. Neither one of us said a word. Who knows? Maybe he would have told me the truth if we'd sat there long enough—or if his cell phone hadn't started ringing.

He fished it out of his briefcase and listened for a half a second. Then he said, "I can't talk right now." The person on the other end of the line said something and Dr. Frazer more or less exploded. "She's what? Where is she?" Then more talk from the other end. "I'll be right there."

He snapped his briefcase shut and headed for the door. Then he turned. "Go home, Felicity. Right now. This whole Grail business is far more dangerous than you or your mother imagine."

Then he was gone.

You're probably wondering why I didn't follow him to the elevator. But I had one last job to do at MBW that afternoon, and it wasn't magical. Not in the least. I closed the door, locked myself in, and started to watch those Grail commercials.

And Mr. Bingley was right. Babies crying because Morgan le Fey soured their milk, Baby Galahad leading the quest for a more intelligent baby cup. There wasn't anything to nourish or inspire the human spirit in those commercials. They were absolutely the opposite of everything the real Grail stood for. But maybe that was the point. In a world where creativity was drying up, where the Grail's power was fading, those commercials might look pretty good.

Concentrate on the here and now.

That's what I had to do. I stared down at my hands. They were solid, real. So was the Grail. Mordred's future was still just that. The future.

I turned everything off and loaded things up— my Grail drawing, the MBW notebook. Then from inside my pack, Dr. Nimuet's crystal clunked against the edge of the table. A handful of Time sparkles shot into the air and my necklace started to glow. I decided to try one last experiment.

The amber and purple lights sucked me right in. Fast. Not back to Mordred's fire, but to some kind of high-tech lab. Bunches and bunches of people were milling around, and every single one of them was wearing something like a space suit with goggles and gloves. Behind them, this wall of glass or plastic—something hard and clear anyway—blocked off a narrow room. A spotless white counter stretched across one wall. And positioned exactly in the center of the counter was that old bronze chest, the one I'd seen before—in my visions.

The chest that held the Grail.

A door opened and a uniformed technician, carrying a camera and tripod, moved toward the box. Everybody in the lab stopped what they were doing to watch. The technician set the camera on the counter, then fumbled with the tripod. You just knew it was impossible to set that thing up with a pair of astronaut mitts on your hands. Finally, the technician pulled them off.

"Hey, Blessing," somebody yelled. "Do you think that's safe?"

"Watch what you're doing there, Amanda!" somebody else called out.

The technician—Amanda—just waved and said, "It's okay." Her voice had a muffled, closed-in kind of sound.

In seconds, the tripod was positioned directly in front of the chest. So was the camera. Then Amanda pulled back the hood on her uniform and peeled off her goggles. She looked like one of Mom's graduate students. Long, wavy brown hair. Soft, dark eyes. The girl checked the camera settings again, made a few adjustments, then headed toward the chest.

You could feel the tension rising in the lab—even my necklace started to glow. And at exactly that moment, I heard them. The Grail creatures, their joyous song. I even heard the Grail goddess, her voice higher, clearer, fuller than the rest. But apparently, nobody heard this but me. And nobody seemed to see what happened next—a swirl of amber and purple lights burst from the chest just as Amanda lifted the lid.

It swung back and someone shouted, "Careful, Amanda!"

She nodded, then slowly, slowly, slowly, reached into the chest.

"Stop!" Someone else yelled as a door slammed open.

"Stop her!" It was Dr. Frazer. But he was too late.

A blinding light shot out of the box. A scream. Amanda Blessing's empty hands, her bleeding hands. More screams.

Dr. Frazer ran down the stairs. He grabbed a pair of goggles and mitts, then raced into the Grail room. "Call an ambulance," he shouted.

A cluster of technicians gathered around him. "It's her hands," he was saying through all those screams. Amanda Blessing's screams. "The skin's burned right off."

"Her eyes," a woman cried. "My god, look at her eyes."

And then I was back in the conference room, feeling like all the life had been sucked right out of me, my necklace burning red-hot against my skin.

"What did you expect, Grail Keeper?" Mordred laughed. "The Grail's more than a harmless bauble. Much more." He picked up Dr. Nimuet's crystal and tossed it like a tennis ball in his hand.

"So now you're wondering why the Grail burned that girl. You're wondering if it will burn you."

I backed away, trying to hide my thoughts—because he was right.

Mordred came closer. He shoved the crystal toward my face. "Here, consult this puny little wonder. *See* your future."

I couldn't help myself. The sparkles cleared and I was in the lab again. But so was Mom . . . All pale and shaky, staring through goggled eyes at that bronze box.

Mom.

And then for some reason, Dr. Frazer's voice was playing through my head.

She's what? Where is she? I'll be right there.

He'd been talking about Mom. I shook my head, willing the vision away. "Where is this place? Tell me."

Mordred laughed again. "You're too late, Grail Keeper. And too weak."

My necklace glowed hotter, brighter. I tried peering back into Dr. Nimuet's crystal. Surely it would show me.

Show me.

Mordred heard my thought and started to shake the crystal. Hard. Really hard. Then he swung back and hurled it against the far wall.

It shattered and burst into amber and purple flames.

But just for a split second, I'd *Seen* what I wanted to know. And I raced toward the elevator.

It took over half an hour to get to Dr. Gildas's Museum of Antiquities—a gray, dismal old building with long narrow windows and crumbling gargoyles. A pair of those armed New Knights of the Round Table blocked my way.

"The museum is closed until tomorrow morning," one of them said. "Come back then."

"But I'm here to meet my mother. She's inside with Dr. Frazer."

Neither guard blinked. They just looked straight ahead at the office building across the street.

"It'll only take a minute," I added.

Absolutely no reaction—except that my necklace had really heated up. It felt warm and heavy against my skin. Magic working overtime, I guess. Because still the guards didn't blink. I stood on tiptoe and waved my hands in front of their eyes—and nothing happened. They just stood there, like those gargoyles perched on the front of the building, hypnotized or something. So I dashed inside.

The central hall was empty—dark and kind of seedy. The whole place smelled like a storm cellar back home. Damp, wet, and mildewy. Every step I took echoed like crazy, so I took my shoes off and started toward the back of the building.

Then my necklace warmed up again. The amber stones actually glowed. They were throwing off light and I could see through the gloom: the exhibits of medieval shoes on my left, the Roman bath display on my right. But there was more. I suddenly *knew* the door to that lab was going to be past the hall of armor and to the left.

That's when I got this really crazy idea.

If Mom was a Grail Keeper like me, then why couldn't I communicate with her, like I did with Morgan le Fey and even Mordred? So I cleared my mind, and sent out a thought.

Mom. Are you still here?

No answer.

I sent out the same thought over and over and over again. *Are you still here? Are you still here? Are you still here?*

The hall got darker, quieter. Even with my necklace, I could just barely make out the individual suits of armor lined up along either wall. It felt like dozens of invisible eyes were watching me through dozens of rusty visors. Then, suddenly, just past the last towering armored horse and rider, I heard voices. A couple of guys talking.

"That's one mouthy redhead," a voice said.

"What do you expect from a female Yank?"

No doubt about it. Mom *was* there.

The two guards were blocking the door, balancing rifles across their arms. I stepped out of the shadows, and before either one could say another word, their eyes locked on to my necklace. Then, in seconds, they were both completely zoned out. All I had to do was slip on my shoes, edge around the guards, and start down those stairs to the basement.

It was exactly like that vision in Dr. Nimuet's crystal—clean, bright, well lighted. Totally different from the rest of the museum—and probably why it had been "closed for repairs": so Dr. Gildas could put this lab together. A thrum of computers, the click of people working at keyboards. My necklace glowed bright, bright, bright. With each step, I was getting closer to Mom, closer to the Grail. I sent out another message.

Mom. Mom.

"Don't go any closer!"

It was Mom, and she clamped a pair of those goggles onto my head.

"See what you've done now?" she cried.

At first, I thought she was mad at me. I mean, it's hard to tell when the person doing the talking is also wearing goggles. Then I realized she was yelling at Dr. Frazer and Miss Nimuet, who were suddenly standing right behind me.

Everybody in the lab stopped working and looked up at us through their goggles. "Calm down, Vanessa," Dr. Frazer said. He led Mom and me into a corner behind the stairs. Miss Nimuet followed close behind.

"Calm down?" Mom snapped. "Not until I know the whole truth. You can't even photograph that thing, can you?" She nodded toward the chest behind the glass.

The Grail chest.

I turned to get a closer look. And despite Amanda Blessing, despite everything—I felt this weird connection, a need to walk into that little room, open that box, and take out the Grail. Miss Nimuet touched my hand lightly, and to this day I'm not sure about this, but I think she said, "You have nothing to fear." Well, that yanked me back to reality.

"We've been over this already," Dr. Frazer was saying. "The Grail's apparently impossible to photograph. One of Archie's technicians . . ." His voice broke and he looked away.

That explained a lot. Amanda Blessing. The blank slides.

Amanda Blessing. Who's Amanda Blessing?

Mom's voice—in my head.

I flashed back the answer, without words. *Without words.* Mom stripped off her goggles and stared at me.

How are you telling me this?

Miss Nimuet edged closer, her eyes suddenly bright and sharp. I swear a bunch of Time Shimmers shot out of her hat. "What has Felicity told you, Vanessa? What have you *Seen*?"

Mom's face went absolutely ashen, and her eyes latched on to mine. "Amanda Blessing. Burned. Blind." She touched my cheek. "How do you know this?" she whispered. "How did you tell me this?"

Well, what could I say? I just shook my head and tried to close off my thoughts so Mom wouldn't freak out again.

And that's when I heard them—the Grail voices, calling to me, just like they had in Dr.

Nimuet's crystal. They were soft and friendly, not scary or threatening. My necklace tingled against my skin, and for the first time, I *understood* their voices.

Take us home. Take us home, Grail Keeper.

I must have taken a step or two toward the Grail, because Mom's hands suddenly dug into my shoulders, and I couldn't move. Her voice was all fire.

"Why did you let me put Felicity at risk this way?" she shouted, looking first at Dr. Frazer, then Miss Nimuet. "Why didn't you tell me the truth from the beginning?"

Dr. Frazer took off his goggles. His face was whiter than Mom's. "I merely suspected its full power—until yesterday. Then I told you to stay away."

The Grail voices grew louder. *Take us home. Take us home.*

But I turned away, suddenly afraid to listen.

Because I'd remembered something else, a tiny shred of memory. The charm. There in the tunnel when Dr. Gildas had found the Grail, he was just about to lift it out of that bronze chest when a voice, Mordred's voice, had cried, *Wait, you old fool! Use the charm!*

And I didn't know the words. The charm used a magic I didn't know.

Mom moved toward the stairs, taking me with her.

"You're a medievalist, Vanessa," Dr. Frazer was saying. He paused, then his words came out slow, careful. "You know the Grail legend as well as I do."

Mom stopped just as we reached the first step. She turned around and looked at the Grail box. The guards crossed and crisscrossed the walled-off room. Mom's hands began to tremble. Her lower lip quivered. Something had scared her. But what?

Those who look upon the Grail without clarity of vision shall go mad or die—Mom's voice in my head again.

Then a flood of thoughts came rushing into my brain. Did that mean I was crazy? I mean, maybe all those Grail visions were a form of madness: the Shimmer of Time, the raven-haired boy, even Morgan le Fey.

What are you thinking?

I looked at Mom.

I'm hearing your thoughts! her mind flashed. *It's starting again!*

She grabbed my arm and pulled me up the first two or three steps. Miss Nimuet charged after us. "Don't jump to conclusions, Vanessa."

Which made me think that Miss Nimuet was reading both of our minds. Then everything started happening too fast. I couldn't think straight. Mom pushed me toward the door and tore off my goggles. Dr. Frazer started after us.

"I'll take you home. Please, Vanessa, let's talk this out."

I've been such a fool!

Then Mom's thoughts got all jumbled up. Something about protecting one's young and being a mother and—who knows? We were halfway up when I tried to tell her I could take care of myself. Honestly, I don't know if I said it or thought it. But Mom just kept right on pushing me—up, up toward the door.

We were near the top when Miss Nimuet called out again. "You're making a mistake."

Mom and I stumbled across the top step, and she hurled my goggles into Dr. Frazer's chest. "Keep your nose out of our business, both of you!" she cried, reaching for the door.

The Grail voices grew louder, stronger. *Take us home, take us home, take us home.*

And then the door shut tight.

Chapter 18

An Enormous, Crumbling Old Book

No harm does come to the Maid who Keeps the Grail
if she is Known to the Keepers of Time and the Guardians
of Earth.
—*The Second Book of Nimue,*
from the private collection of Vivian Nimuet

"Tonight we'll book a flight back home," Mom said, tipping the taxi driver, "and pretend none of this ever happened." She got out of the cab and crossed the street to Miss Nimuet's building. But I just sat there, stunned. Like a deer in the headlights.

"Are you all right, miss?" The driver glanced up in the rearview mirror. Cars were honking all around us.

"Oh, right."

I slid across the backseat and closed the door behind me. Traffic was heavy, so it took a while before I could cross the street. That's when I saw Mom—just standing there, kind of tranced-out in front of Miss Nimuet's. And then, from clear across that street full of noise and cars and people, I heard her think this:

No harm does come to the Maid who Keeps the Grail.

I hurried across, but by the time I got there, Mom was herself again, rattling on about frequent flyer miles and whether we should fly into St. Louis or Kansas City.

"Let's stay here," I said. "Through Friday, at least."

The elevator doors opened and I followed Mom inside. "Absolutely not. It's far too dangerous."

Okay, so I admit there was something appealing about not having to face Mordred again or think about the Grail. Because that logical, rational side of my brain kept playing one scene over and over again: Amanda Blessing crumpled on the floor, her screams, and Dr. Frazer. *Her hands. . . . The skin's burned right off.* I stared down at my own. Should I have grabbed the Grail back there? Maybe being burned and blind was the price I'd have to pay to save it. To save Mom, to save myself.

But what would I do with it? Where would I take it? Burned and blind, I wouldn't even make it out of the museum. Maybe the answer was back at MBW after all. If I didn't go back there, I wouldn't have a future. I wouldn't even have a life. Period.

"Let me finish my last assignment for Crystal," I said at last. "Then we can go."

"Don't you understand, Felicity? That thing Ian dug up. It burns people. It blinds them." The elevator jerked to a stop and the doors opened. Mom stood there for a second, blinking into the dark hall. "Who knows?" she whispered. "It might even kill."

She stepped into the hall and took a deep breath. I took one too. Then I said, "You won't have a daughter anymore if we go back now."

Mom turned and stared at me. Like she'd never seen me before, like she was already Raven Head's mother. You could almost hear that kid's mean little laugh and Mordred's snicker: *You're too late . . . too weak.* Is that what he'd meant? That his world was inevitable because Mom would decide to leave London—and I wouldn't be able to convince her to stay?

I conjured up that image of Mordred's black fire, that wasteland of broken Grails, and tried to send it to Mom. But nothing happened, at least that's what I thought at the time. Because she just looked at me like I was a stranger. So I figured the whole mind-reading scene at the museum must have been a fluke caused by the magic of the Grail or Mom's vision thing. Clarity of vision. Maybe sometimes you have it, sometimes you don't.

Then Mom suddenly touched my necklace. "Where did you get this?"

And before I could think of anything believable to say, Mom answered her own question. "Let me guess. Vivian Nimuet. It has her name written all over it." Mom fumbled with the keys and unlocked the door. She went straight into Dr. Nimuet's library and shut herself in for the rest of the afternoon.

I sent an e-mail off to Erin about my latest work on BowWow Dog Chow and Cargill Tummy Soothers. Nothing important, but I thought it might be the last chance I'd get to talk to her, to let her know I was around if. . . . I mean, if Mom took us home, would all my old e-mails get sucked out of her computer the minute Raven Head replaced me? Would Erin forget that Halloween when we dressed up like green Orion slave girls from *Star Trek* or the time I kissed Ryan Baker on a dare?

But I knew the answer.

I'd seen that wasteland, Mordred's black fire. Who knows? In that world, Erin might not even exist.

Then Mom was standing just behind me. "I want to show you something," she said. I followed her into the library.

An enormous, crumbling old book perched on top of the desk. "Vivian Nimuet dropped this off before we went to the museum." Mom ran her fingers over the hand-lettered title: *The Second Book of Nimue.* "She says her father translated this years ago from a fifth-century manuscript."

Slowly, Mom opened the book and a fluttering of amber and purple lights spilled across the desk. She didn't bat an eye. "The illustrations are copies from the original manuscript. Including this one."

She turned to a drawing of a wasteland filled with rocky, broken, yellow Grails. There were thousands of them, stretching across a wide valley; the sky above was low, heavy, and dark. A mountain loomed in the distance.

You've Seen this before? Mom's thought.

I nodded.

Just as I feared. Mom was shaking all over. *Just as I knew.*

"You've *Seen* this too?" I asked. "Before now?"

Mom crumpled into a chair. "Your great-grandmother was a painter. Her last painting, the one she willed to me . . . It was this very scene."

I started shaking too. "You never showed me that painting."

Tears were streaming down Mom's face, and for a long time, she didn't say anything. Finally, she wiped her cheeks and stared down into her hands. "I burned it. Right after she died."

"Why?"

"Because she told me . . ." Mom stopped and her thoughts came rushing into mine. Perfect clarity of vision. *Because she told me that this was the future without my daughter.*

I sank into the sofa. Great-grandmother had died before I was born. I never even knew her. How could she know about the Grail, Mordred's wasteland, me? Unless . . .

Unless she was a Grail Keeper too.

And then everything started making total sense. All those déjà vu moments. Morgan le Fey's explanations about a family of women. Even Mom's comment back at the lab: *It's starting again.* Mom and Great-grandmother. They'd probably heard each other's thoughts, like Morgan le Fey and me . . . like Mordred and me . . . like Mom and me.

"Why didn't you tell me?" By this time, I was crying too. "Why didn't you tell me all this ESP stuff ran in the family?"

"I didn't believe it myself." Mom got up and started walking around the room. "Part of me thought I'd just imagined it all. Anyway, that's what your dad liked to think—what he wanted me to think."

She went back to Dr. Nimuet's book and turned the next page. There was a drawing of a man, dark and slight, standing before a billowing black fire. Mordred's fire. Underneath the picture, Dr. Nimuet had written these words: *And he of Arthur's line may purge the world of Light unless he is prevented.*

"I have to go back to MBW," I said. "Regardless."

Mom touched my necklace again. "What did you mean out in the hall? You know, about me not having a daughter?"

And in a flash, the raven-haired boy burst into the library. He hurled Merlin on the floor, laughing as the old cat squealed in pain.

"My god," Mom whispered. "That boy. He's back."

"If we leave London now," I said, "he's your son."

And I swear, he looked right at me and grinned. Just like Mordred. That bright, smug, awful grin. Then he chased Merlin into the hall.

"My son," Mom said slowly. "Who's his father?" She looked at me almost like she hoped I wouldn't know.

I pointed to the picture of Mordred. "He of Arthur's line."

With shaking hands, Mom turned to another page in Dr. Nimuet's book. "This passage has been haunting me all day," she said softly. "'No harm does come to the Maid who Keeps the Grail if she is Known to the Keepers of Time. . . .'" Mom's voice trailed off. "Do they know you? Are you the Maid?"

I looked down at my hands. They had gone transparent, as clear as glass. "Even if I'm not, what do I have to lose?"

Chapter 19

Above the Mist

The boat began to glide through the mists. Swiftly and surely . . . [it] poled through the thick and clinging damp. . . ."
—Marion Zimmer Bradley,
The Mists of Avalon

Morgan le Fey was waiting for me in Miss Nimuet's old room. All the lights were out, and she was standing by the window in a long white gown, staring down at the street. She turned and Merlin was in her arms.

He jumped from hers into mine. "Why didn't you tell me?" I asked.

"Tell you what?" She stroked the soft spot under Merlin's chin. He nipped her fingertips.

"About Mom and Great-grandmother."

Irrelevant. Her thought.

How can you say that? My thought.

171

Merlin leaped from my arms and scampered down the hall.

"This is what matters now," Morgan le Fey said softly. She gestured down at the street, the darkened, joyless street.

She'd been right about the theater—it was boarded up, a ghostly outline against the street lights. The twenty-four-hour music store two doors down was dark too, and the Indian restaurant in between, which usually had people lined up outside its doors, looked deserted. With each passing minute, Mordred's world was becoming more real, mine was slipping away.

Actually, we were both fading. Morgan le Fey's white gown was like a sheer, see-through curtain at a nighttime window; my arms and hands and legs were perfectly clear. I'd lost count of all the times my body had faded in and out.

"How much time do we have left?" I asked.

"Concentrate on more immediate matters," she snapped back. "Have you a plan? What will you do on Friday to secure the Grail?"

Her question cut to the chase. But something was wrong. Way wrong. I mean, Morgan le Fey was asking me what to do. So I said, "Don't you have a plan of your own?"

Her mind went blank—and not because she was screening her thoughts. She didn't have a single trick left up her sleeve! So much for her so-called sorcery.

Your attitude is not becoming, she thought.

Neither is yours, I fired back.

So we just stood there watching each other fade in and out, sensing that time, even life itself was seeping deep into that abyss—toward Mordred's black fire. Finally, that awful transparency passed and Morgan le Fey lightly touched my arm.

"Surely," she said, "you have worked long enough in Mordred's workshop to learn the craft of advertising."

I shook my head. "I didn't write any commercials, if that's what you mean." Then I remembered my drawing, the beautiful Grail drawing. *Perhaps the magic of my necklace . . .*

Morgan le Fey laughed bitterly. "The magic in your necklace flows from the past, from Avalon. Its magic cannot touch on matters so completely bound to the here and now."

So I'm totally alone. No magic can help me.

Well, that came as a shock. Not so much that magic couldn't help me, but that I wanted it. For the first time in my life, I wanted magic, I wanted to be magical.

But you are magical.

Morgan le Fey's thought didn't sound convincing. None of her thoughts did. Not anymore.

I backed away. Without the power of that necklace, was I any more magical than Amanda Blessing? Her burned hands, her blinded eyes?

Morgan le Fey pretended not to *See* my fear, but suddenly I could *See* hers. Talk about clarity of vision! Everything became crystal clear—she couldn't *See* beyond tomorrow. She had lost control of me . . . and the future. We stood face to face. Had I grown somehow? We seemed to be exactly the same height.

"I must leave you to your own devices," Morgan le Fey whispered. Then the Time Shimmers appeared and she slipped through their doorway.

I spent the next morning obsessing over magic potions or some spell that would *show* me what to do, wishing with all my heart that Mordred hadn't smashed Dr. Nimuet's paperweight. I even asked Mom to search the *Second Book of Nimue* for the words to that charm, the one Dr. Gildas and maybe even Mordred had used back in the tunnel. But there wasn't a single reference in the whole book to a charm—any charm. In desperation, I called Dr. Frazer. Maybe he knew. But he wasn't in.

By noon, my strategy had shifted. I was off magic and on to advertising. I switched on the TV to watch commercials. Until then, I'd never really *watched* them, the commercials, I mean, instead of the shows.

And it was way too entertaining.

Because the shows, every single one of them, were American re-runs—including a soap opera I used to watch with Erin. *The Sands of Time.* No kidding. So the ads looked terrific. Even the ones for BowWow Dog Chow and Cargill's Tummy Soothers. I called Mom in to watch and she handed me a very thin *London Times.* Its front page story:

CREATIVE MALAISE SWEEPS COUNTRY

THE ARTS HIT HARD; BBC ALL BUT SHUTS DOWN

I fired off an e-mail to Erin and waited. Was the same thing happening back home? An hour crept by, crammed with dog chow and Tummy Soother commercials, then another and another. Finally, a reply from Erin: "Lots of re-runs, including *Sands.* Who cares? Just ordered one of those Grails for Aunt Sarah's baby. Very cool."

And no lie, at just that moment, Mom called me back to the TV, which was playing the MBW baby Grail commercial, complete with Infant Sir Galahad, lots of sour milk, plus a toll free number and Web address for advance orders.

Mom and I stared at the screen. The commercial played again and again. And every time it looked a little better, a little less offensive. No wonder Erin had ordered one. Finally, I switched off the TV.

"Dr. Gildas and Mr. Bingley must have caved in," I whispered. Which made me wonder if that meeting the next day would matter anymore. Because all I could hear was Mordred's words in my head.

You're too late, Grail Keeper. And too weak.

Still I couldn't give up. Not yet. I mean, would you? So I set to work on a new idea for a baby Grail campaign, whether anybody cared or not. At first, I tried working with Mom in the library. But neither of us could concentrate. Raven Head kept appearing, barging in, tearing pages out of books or tormenting Merlin. Then I tried moving around. By suppertime, I'd worked in every single room in the flat. Still, he followed me everywhere—into the kitchen, the dining room,

Mom's bedroom. He smashed china, tore the curtains down in the sitting room, and ripped up Mom's mattress with his pocketknife. Sure, all this happened in his world, not ours. But it was like his was becoming realer and realer and realer. Plus, every time Mom and I saw him, I'd go transparent—and Mom would go as white as Ivory soap.

Finally, we had supper. Who knows what we ate? It just tasted gray and sort of lumpy. "I'm going with you tomorrow," Mom announced as we cleared the table. And I was glad. At least if I did completely fade away at MBW, she'd be with me right up until the very end.

At midnight, I gave up and went to bed.

Then suddenly I jerked awake. She was back— Morgan le Fey, stepping through the bedroom wall at Maiden's Cottage. Now I should have known something was up. I mean, Maiden's Cottage? But I didn't have time to think because Morgan le Fey said, "You have a plan, I assume." Just like the night before.

But this time, I did.

I jumped out of bed and crossed the hall to Mom's room. She was asleep but somehow that didn't stop me. I motioned for Morgan le Fey and together we glided across the rug to the old

177

wardrobe in the corner. Mom's white linen suit, the one she always wears when she has to make a big speech or something, was hanging on the door.

"All you have to do," I whispered, "is come to the meeting tomorrow."

I remember thinking Morgan le Fey would have to be perfect—jewelry, hair, makeup. And I also remember how bright everything looked, almost unreal. When I turned around, Morgan le Fey was wearing Mom's suit and looking as if it had been made for her. It was perfect except that the suit kind of glowed in the dark.

"It always happens thus in a dream," she said.

Okay, I should have known. But haven't you had those dreams that seem so real somehow that you don't really have a clue until you wake up?

Anyway, Morgan le Fey started lecturing me, as usual. "Things never happen this smoothly in the waking world. You, of all people, should know that." She unbuttoned Mom's jacket. "Nevertheless, a dream can sometimes be a beginning."

Suddenly, the room clouded over and I was pulled out of one dream and into another. Into a place that seemed familiar. Had I dreamed this dream before? I honestly don't know. But there was mist or fog everywhere, dense and mysterious but comforting too. And my necklace (which I was somehow wearing) lit the way.

As my necklace broke through all the gloom, I started to hear this gentle lapping sound, maybe even an oar dipping in and out of water. Then a hand was pulling me out of the mist and into a swirl of Time Shimmers. I could just make out the outline of Morgan le Fey.

"Come, Felicity," she said. "Above the mist."

"Where am I?" Beyond the glow of my necklace, everything was still pretty dark.

"You are in Avalon."

"Am I really here or is this a dream too?"

"You are as truly in Avalon as one from your world may ever be," Morgan le Fey said softly.

The mist suddenly cleared as a full moon cut through the darkness. We were standing in an orchard, all silver in the moonlight, the trees heavy with apples.

And then I had an idea—a real *eureka!* kind of idea.

Chapter 20

A Really Dark Kind of Drama

There is an inherent drama in every product.
—Leo Burnett

So the next morning, there we were. Mom, wearing her white pantsuit, and me crammed into the elevator with Crystal and a bunch of other MBW people on the way up to the twenty-first floor.

Does Ms. DuLac always look this eccentric? Mom's thought.

Pretty much. My thought. Although I had to admit Crystal had outdone herself. She was more or less wrapped up in this long blue drapey thing, something you'd see in a really old painting.

Very Pre-Raphaelite. That was Mom again.

She was really getting into nonverbal communication. But at that very instant, Crystal turned and smiled at both of us. Like she'd *heard* it too. So Mom said something nice about the ropes of amber beads dangling around Crystal's neck.

"They're Victorian, of course," she said. "Pre-Raphaelite, you might say."

Well, that made me do a double take. Then the doors opened and we were there.

"Oh, my god," Mom gasped. She stared into the darkness for a moment as the people on the elevator pushed past her. All that black and gleaming red, the Pendragon towering over us on the opposite wall.

"This isn't right, Felicity. We shouldn't be here." Mom started nudging me back to the elevator. So it was my turn to do the ESP thing.

We have no choice. Remember?

Well, that stopped her. But so did Crystal, which made me wonder again. . . .

"Please don't worry, Dr. Jones. Everyone, just *everyone*, has this reaction the first time they're here. Mr. Mordreaut has a morbid decorator. That's all." Crystal squinted through her tiny wire-framed glasses, then started down the hall. "This way," she said.

We were about halfway to the conference room when Mom suddenly asked, "What's that smell?"

How could I have forgotten? I mean, my amber necklace felt warm against my skin, so it was hard at work, neutralizing all those wicked vapors. Why hadn't I thought to get Mom some protection? I should have asked Morgan le Fey for one of her potions or something. Because by the time we'd reached the conference room, Mom was looking green.

"Where's the restroom?" she asked.

I started to pull Mom back toward the elevator, because she'd need more than a bathroom, she'd need fresh air. But Crystal stopped me. "I'll take care of your mum, Felicity," she said.

So I walked toward the conference room alone. Voices drifted down the hall. "Record-breaking sales. . . ." "A million orders in the first three hours. . . ." "What do I know about advertising?"

That last was Mr. Bingley, which made me wonder again if I was already too late. Nobody would care about my advertising campaign anymore. Nobody needed it. I kind of hovered in the doorway. The room was full of people—a bunch from Royal Regal and MBW, Dr. Gildas, and even Dr. Frazer. His back was turned to me and he was bending over something. Just what, I couldn't tell. Then I heard Mr. Bingley say, "But with the right campaign, advance orders could hit ten million a day!"

That was all the encouragement I needed.

I backed away and unlocked a supply closet with my MBW ID. It was perfectly dark inside.

I took a deep breath, closed my eyes again, touched my necklace, and thought.

Morgan le Fey. It's time.

When I opened my eyes, there she was—in a shower of Time Shimmers.

"I told you I would come," she said.

All that purple and amber light gave off this magical kind of glow there in the darkness. I could see her perfectly—and she looked magnificent, like a character on the cover of a fantasy book. Mr. Bingley would be impressed. But what about Mordred?

Morgan le Fey answered my thought. "As you suggested, I created a diversion for him in Camelot. He will not be here today."

Now you're probably thinking, Wow, what a relief!

But that's not how I felt at all.

I felt *magical*. Absolutely, positively magical.

"Let's go," I said, cracking open the door.

By the time we got to the conference room, I had started hearing Grail voices again. And they were friendly—so clear and sweet and pure. I wasn't one bit afraid. Not anymore. All the worries I'd had—even the ones about Amanda Blessing—they went right out of my head. I took Morgan le Fey's hand, and together we walked into the room.

The minute we crossed the threshold, the Grail voices stopped. In fact, the whole room went quiet, and everybody just stared at Morgan le Fey. Her gold crown shimmered in the spotlights. Grail creatures, embroidered in fine gold thread, spiraled up her amber gown and purple cloak. Her hair sparkled like polished copper beneath yards and yards of sheer silken veils. I told you she was magnificent!

Then I took a step forward. "May I present Royal Regal's new spokeswoman, Morganna Fey as Thomas Malory's Lady of the Lake." Still, the room was quiet. Finally, I said, "What do you think, Mr. Bingley?"

He just sat there a minute longer, his eyes popping out of his head. He took a deep breath. "This is *great*!"

Then the whole room broke into applause. Even Dr. Gildas stood up and clapped. Dr. Frazer was clapping too.

"I wouldn't have believed it," he said, "but you may have stolen our thunder." He lightly touched a bronze box right in front of him.

The bronze box.

For an instant, I was back in that tunnel again, watching Dr. Gildas pry it open, gasping as the amber and purple shimmers escaped, hearing Mordred's voice:

Wait, you old fool!

But it *was* Mordred's voice—in the here and now. He came pushing through the conference room door, dragging Mom and Crystal with him.

"How rude to start a meeting without all the players," Mordred sneered. "Look who I've found." He released Crystal, but his fingers dug into Mom's arm. "The famous Dr. Vanessa Jones, mother to our dear Felicity." Mom's face was as green as before; she was still fighting all that nausea. Already she was beginning to look like the Mom of Mordred's future, defeated and sad.

He pushed Mom toward Dr. Frazer, then crossed to stand right in front of Morgan le Fey and me. His breath was hot on my face.

"I see you've brought us a spokeswoman. I'd expected more originality."

"It is original!" Mr. Bingley was on his feet, yelling across the table. "It'll triple sales. Easily."

But Mordred ignored him, ignored everybody but me—and Morgan le Fey. He moved even closer, and my necklace went red-hot. Morgan le Fey stepped between us. She looked just as pale as Mom, just as green. But there wasn't anything defeated about the way she moved.

"Leave the girl alone. Your fight is with me."

The whole room felt like a stage. Mordred, Morgan le Fey, and I were the actors. Everybody else was just a spectator—even Mom and Crystal, Dr. Frazer and Dr. Gildas. They were watching a play, a really dark kind of drama, and no matter how much they wanted to intervene, they didn't have a part. They couldn't act.

Mordred took a step back and grinned. "This lady looks familiar. Perhaps we've met before." His smile was crooked. "Another place. Another Time."

Morgan le Fey stared back. "Have I surprised you?"

"Not, I think, as much as I've surprised you, my lady."

Mordred started to pace around the table, hands clasped around his back, his eyes fixed on the bronze box. "So it's here at last, I see," he said. His Pendragon ring flashed as his hands reached out for the box.

Suddenly, the spell was broken, and it was like Dr. Frazer had jumped on stage. He pulled the box toward him; his hands rested loosely on the top. "This doesn't belong to you."

Then my head cleared, and the Grail voices were calling to me again: *Now! Take us home now!*

I *Saw* the Grail inside the box. I could clearly see every creature, every leaf, every image etched into its sides, and they were moving across its surface like wild creatures, churning up clouds of purple and amber sparkles.

Mordred sprang back and grabbed my neck. He tore away the top of my sweater. His fingernails cut into my skin.

"She's stronger than you, Morgan!" he cried. "But this necklace won't save her."

Mom gasped and struggled toward me through bunches of MBW people.

"Her life is ebbing away," Mordred went on, digging deeper, deeper into my skin, so deep that his fingers seemed to go right through to the other side.

Mom gasped again—and so did everybody else. Because there in front of all those people, my whole body kind of flickered out. I was as sheer and as flimsy as one of Morgan le Fey's veils. It was like Mordred was willing me into oblivion.

"Your last Grail Keeper is nothing more than a shadow of her former self." Mordred laughed. "In a few hours, she won't even be a memory."

He started to strip away my necklace, but I was faster. Because I *knew* what was coming. The voices told me. So I darted behind the table, then ran to the other side, where Dr. Frazer was still guarding the Grail.

"It won't hurt me," I said.

"Don't let her do it!" Dr. Gildas tripped over Mom, shoved past Crystal. "I'll not be beaten by a child!"

"Nor will I!" Mordred brushed Dr. Gildas out of the way and leaped as neat as a cat over two chairs and onto the table. He towered over Dr. Frazer and me.

"Leave her alone!" Dr. Frazer growled.

I grabbed the box. Mordred kept right on coming.

Then Dr. Frazer picked up a chair and smashed it into Mordred's legs. He crumpled up in pain.

I stepped back against the conference room wall and into somebody's arms. I remember hearing Mom shout, seeing Dr. Frazer crouched over Mordred. Then everything disappeared behind a doorway of furious amber and purple lights.

Chapter 21

Shadows on the Wind

*. . . and she was one of the damosels of the lake, the
hight Nimue.*
—Sir Thomas Malory,
Le Morte D'Arthur

All I could see were sparkles—at first anyway.
They were dancing and shimmering and twirling
around like autumn leaves on a gusty day. They
bounced off my skin, brushed against my face, cir-
cled through my hair. And just like before, they
prickled and tickled and tingled. But this time,
those sparkles were part of *me,* and I was part of
them. And together, we were *flying!* Flying through
this vast, long, dark tunnel of wispy purple clouds.
We were moving forward, forward through . . .

Time?

Anyway, that's what I decided. I was traveling
through Time. So I hugged that bronze box close

190

and tried not to stress. But it was hard not to. I mean, where was I? And where was I going? And who had sent me here? Because I can tell you this: Time travel wasn't any part of any plan I'd made with Morgan le Fey.

Then everything slowed down, and one by one the Time Shimmers flickered out. I was still flying, more or less, but flying solo without those amber and purple lights. Weird as this may sound, I missed them. Never in my life had I felt so alone.

Thin, purple clouds brushed against my face like cobwebs. I strained to hear the Grail voices. They were silent. I looked down at the bronze box in my arms. It wasn't there! I mean, I could feel it, but I couldn't *See* it—or anything else for that matter. My arms, my hands, my legs. Sure I could feel them, but maybe I'd just grown used to the habit of feeling. Maybe they didn't exist. Maybe I didn't exist. Well, that freaked me out. So I tried to *think things through.* This was Time travel, I told myself. It wasn't easy. Ever. So maybe all this freakiness was normal. Besides, what did I have to worry about? I mean, the Grail box was in my arms. I could *feel* it. Right?

Then, all of a sudden, this great big wind rushed through the tunnel. It almost stripped the box from my arms, but I held on tight. The wind whirled me around and around and around—still forward somehow, toward this tiny, tiny little pinpoint of light far, far, far away.

The wind tugged at the box in my arms, pulling it loose inch by inch. Had Mordred sent me here? Was the wind his magic? I shook a whole cluster of clouds from my face and wrapped the box tighter, closer in my arms.

That was just before the Time Shimmers returned. And was I ever glad to see them, to feel part of something again! They kind of brought me back to life. I mean, I could see: my legs, my arms, the gleam of the box. Everything was real again. But I also began to make out other shapes, other shadows. Some reminded me of Grail creatures, coiled up like sleeping snakes. Others were definitely human—tall or short, fat or thin—all rushing past like shadows on the wind. And there were whispers, voices maybe—people calling out to one another, their words stripped away by wind and Time.

I am behind you, Felicity. Do not fear.

That was a real voice! Or was it a thought?

Tumbling, tumbling through that wind, I looked back over my shoulder. A woman was following me! Her shape was all misty and dim, but I could *see* her. And in a flash, I knew.

Crystal!

The ghostly voices grew louder, and that pin-point of light ahead got bigger, brighter. The wind sucked the breath right out of my body. I couldn't breathe. I couldn't move. My arms went weak. The box was slipping, slipping away. And my necklace, the amber, it was tingling, growing hot, unbearably hot. I couldn't hold on . . . I couldn't endure. . . .

And then it was over.

I stepped out of a solid stone wall into a dark-ening twilight.

At first, I just lay huddled against the wall, weak and tired. Voices came to me in some crazy for-eign language. Hoofbeats struck a fast rhythm against stone. But I could hear more familiar sounds too: dogs barking, chickens cackling. Was I on a farm?

Finally, my eyes adjusted to the darkness, and there I was: in a courtyard behind a low hedge. On the other side, four hefty women in long dresses moved across the cobblestones. They car-ried platters piled high with savory-smelling meats, a smoky, rich, earthy kind of smell. But then, this whole world smelled different. All around me the air was thicker, sweeter, cleaner.

Never in all my life had I breathed in such pure, wonderful air. . . .

Except . . . except that one time . . . at Chalice Well.

Which meant, of course, that maybe, just maybe, I was either back in Avalon or . . .

And then this page like you read about in *Ivanhoe* or something came running down the stairs, shouting at the women. He stood there gesturing and pointing until they all started toward a castle. A stone castle, the one I'd seen in that vision of the Grail. You remember.

So I was in Camelot. Alone in Camelot.

A tabby cat who looked a lot like Merlin strolled out of the hedge. He brushed up against my leg and purred. Just like Merlin always did. He didn't seem at all surprised to find a stranger from the Twenty-first Century slumped against his historic old hedge. Well, in a way, that cat steadied my nerves. Cats were cats. People were people—no matter which century they came from. Still, I must have stood out like a sore thumb. I mean, a torn sweater, short skirt, and platform shoes aren't exactly medieval.

Merlin's twin meowed and twitched his tail. He was irresistible. I propped the bronze box against the hedge and scooped the cat into my arms. He even smelled like Merlin. But then he twisted away and yowled—because at just that moment, a doorway of Time Shimmers opened and out stepped . . .

Crystal?

I scooped up the Grail box and started to run. But I didn't get far. Because the minute I looked over my shoulder to see if she was going to chase me, she didn't. And maybe it wasn't even Crystal. I mean, she was wearing Crystal's outrageous outfit with all those amber beads, but she'd stripped off her glasses. Her eyes looked wise, *very* wise. Familiar too.

"Miss Nimuet?" I asked.

She brushed the cat out of her way. "I am Nimue in this world, chief counsel to King Arthur." Her voice wasn't flighty like Crystal's or cozy like Miss Nimuet's. It was full of power and authority. In a way, she sounded a lot like Morgan le Fey. Nimue moved closer. "Are you still feeling the effects of Time travel?"

I took a step back. Nimue, or whoever she was, certainly didn't look weak or ill from her trip through that windy, cloudy tunnel. Could I trust her? I mean, as Crystal she'd worked for Mordred.

What do you think?

Her thought rushed into my head, and I just stood there, clutching the box and staring at her. It was not the kind of thought I would have expected from her kind, because she didn't *tell* me to trust her or order me around (like Morgan le Fey, for instance). Instead, she was leaving things up to me, and I liked that, respected that. I decided to trust her.

She pulled me back into the shadows as more serving women walked by. This time, they were carrying baskets of fruit, bread, and pastries—sweet and spicy.

"I'm sorry we couldn't prepare you for this," Nimue whispered. "Bringing you to Camelot was not what either Morgan or I had envisioned."

"The two of you are in this together?"

She nodded. "We haven't much time. Follow me!" She'd unlaced her red high-heeled boots and kicked them off. Then she pointed to the dim outline of a tower. "It will be safe for you there. Follow me."

Nimue darted across the far corner of the courtyard. The page had come back, but his back was turned and he was taking orders from an old guy wearing lots of gold jewelry: a necklace shaped kind of like mine, earrings, and a massive chain. I figured the two of them were so deep in conversation that they'd never notice me. So I wrapped my arms around the Grail box and dashed after Nimue. My timing was perfect.

"We're lucky that tomorrow is Pentecost," Nimue said as I crouched next to her. "Cai and his people are too busy to notice us."

"Cai?" I asked. "As in Sir Cai?" I suddenly remembered this scene from *Sword in the Stone*. Cai was King Arthur's foster brother, and he'd lied about taking that sword out of the stone, but Arthur had forgiven him.

"Over there with the page," Nimue nodded. "That's him. Has a terrible temper, Sir Cai." Then she was moving again, this time behind a cart stacked high with straw. It was hard to keep up. No wonder Miss Nimuet had been so spry!

Which made me ask, "How can you be two— no, three—people at once?"

When we were safe behind the cart, Nimue said, "I am never three people at once. I am always myself." She darted toward a narrow gate that opened into an even narrower passageway.

The Grail box was starting to feel heavy. I'd broken out in a sweat and my ankles felt like they were going to snap in two. Halfway to the gate, I kicked off my shoes and left them there. So somebody back in the fifth or sixth century or whatever is wearing a really fabulous pair of shoes.

Anyway, once inside the passageway, Nimue started talking again. "I learned the magic of disguise from Merlin." She lit a lantern and lifted it just enough to throw a flicker of light down the passageway. "He also taught me the secrets of Time travel. He was a true master, the best of us. In your world, we passed as Merlin Nimuet and his daughter Vivian." She stopped and looked into the darkness. There was nothing but shadow ahead. "Do you sense any danger, Felicity?"

Wow. *She* was asking *me*. I took a deep breath, closed my eyes, and concentrated. *Nothing but darkness*.

"Good," Nimue said.

We hurried down a narrow, clammy passageway. Did you know that stone walls sweat? It's like they create their own weather. And the damp on the floors absolutely soaked through my socks. So there I was, hot and sweaty—and then cold. But I held on to that Grail box; in fact, it was beginning to feel like part of my body, as natural as my arms and legs or the beating of my heart.

Which made me think about what had happened back there in the conference room, the way I'd gone transparent in front of everybody.

In Camelot, in the past, I felt solid and real; none of this phasing in and phasing out. That gave me hope. If I was real in the past, maybe there was still hope for the future.

Nimue stopped. "There are eight steps here. See?" She held the lantern up. Ahead there was a stone stairway leading through a pair of arches. "You go first."

Well, why me? Who knows, but again I thought this was a good sign. Nimue believed in me, so I believed in myself. I got to the top and waited for her. That's when my skin started to tingle; my necklace was warming up again. Without saying a word, we both just *knew*. Some-one was coming—through the second arch. Nimue put out the light, and we backed into a little space behind the first arch. In seconds, we heard footsteps, then voices.

"All this ado for one daffish cat," a man was saying. He held a candle against the dark. "Thrice in five days have we sought this beast thus."

So much for that crazy foreign language I'd heard at first. Somehow my necklace was letting me make some sense of it.

"Ah, Husband!" the woman complained. "Suf-fer us all a thousand deaths if her ladyship and her beloved pet are not reconciled this night."

Nimue held a finger to her lips; her eyes gleamed at mine through the shadows.

"On to the courtyard, Wife, lest the queen cries for Lancelot," the man said. "For sooth, if the lady discovers that her fair knight is absent, lo, our lives shall be a misery."

The two of them rattled on down the steps. Finally, the light from their candle disappeared around a corner. But still we waited in the dark, to be sure they weren't coming back.

And then Nimue lit the lantern again. Who can say how she managed it? One moment there was darkness, the next there was light. It must have been magic.

Like your necklace, I heard her think.

Nimue led me down one more short passageway. She stopped in front of this huge, thick, bulky wooden door. Reaching into her pocket, she took out a key, unlocked the door, and pulled me inside. A steep, rickety-looking stairway spiraled around and around and around. I couldn't see all the way to the top.

"We're safe here. Let's rest a moment, shall we?"

I agreed. Those steps looked pretty wicked, and my whole body felt absolutely wasted. My arms were numb. I sank onto one of the steps, and balanced the Grail box on my lap. The light from the lantern flickered, but I could see Nimue clearly. Her face, her eyes, her skin—smooth and flawless as a model's. How could she have been Miss Nimuet? Had she tricked Mordred too?

Yes, came her answer.

And I remembered that line from Morgan le Fey: *On all of us—save one—it works as a repellent.* Nimue was immune to that nasty cologne Mordred always wore.

Then she laughed, like it was a private joke or something. "I don't think Mordred had a clue. Not until now—when I sent you and me flying through Time."

"So you must have rigged my computer—that valley of broken grails, Mordred's fire."

She nodded. "I knew you needed to see the future we're fighting. Plus it brought you and your mother together, didn't it?" Nimue laughed again.

"Did you discover Time travel?" I asked.

"Oh, no. It was Merlin." Her voice grew soft, her eyes got misty. "I believe now that he anticipated all of this. Mordred's treachery, his mastery of Time travel. But enough talk."

Almost instantly she was moving again—fast. So far ahead that her lantern's light was no more than a pale sliver of color. I tightened my grip on the Grail box and started after her. But I couldn't shake the questions forming in the back of my mind. Mordred. Merlin. Morgan le Fey. Wasn't there something about Nimue too?

Her lantern shimmered, sending shadows dancing across the two of us. Higher and higher and higher we climbed. The passageway narrowed; damp brushed through my sweater. I shivered.

Mordred. Merlin. Morgan le Fey. Nimue. All those names were magical. All those characters— no, *people*—had special powers to use for good . . . or evil. I shivered again because then I remembered. In a paper Mom had written, Merlin had been sealed up in a cave by an ambitious, thieving maiden named—

"I did *not* lock Merlin away to steal his secrets." Nimue turned suddenly on the step in front of me. "Surely you've learned by now that all the women in Camelot wear two faces, one good, one bad."

Then she was climbing again, even faster than before. And this time, she left me no choice. I could either stay in the dark—or follow. So I followed. Up, up, up. The stairs got steeper, narrower too. By then, the Grail box was heavy as lead. But my arms didn't really ache anymore—they just felt like old elastic, stretched out and sloppy.

"Just one more flight," Nimue said, pausing on the last landing. She turned. "I shouldn't have snapped at you back there. It's just that I've never gotten over the slander. Imagine traveling through hundreds and hundreds of years to find out that your good name has been forever tarnished."

"So what happened—to you and Merlin, I mean?"

She smiled. "Merlin, the cat. He's never liked me. But Merlin, my Merlin . . ." She started climbing again. "He slipped away into Time. That is his prison. That is his cave."

We reached the top and another massive locked door. She took out the same key and fitted it into the lock. Then she turned. "Morgan is more philosophical on these matters than I. She believes that becoming a legend, no matter how unfaithful to the truth of your memory, is better than being forgotten." Nimue unlocked the door and we were inside.

The fire in the fireplace was the room's only light. But even so, it felt safe and cozy, familiar even. Maybe it was the smell of lavender. Or the rows and rows of herbs packed together on bunches of shelves, almost like Mom's books.

But this wasn't Columbia, Missouri. It was Camelot.

I walked to the window and looked outside. It was dark mostly, except for a ribbon of turquoise above the horizon and dozens of torchlights flickering like lightning bugs.

"You may set the Grail there."

I turned as Nimue pointed to the table in front of the fireplace.

She must have felt me hesitate. It wasn't that I didn't trust her, it was just that the Grail box had become part of me. It was part of my past, a connection now to my own world.

Do as you see fit.

Nimue's voice in my head. She was giving me another one of her choices. . . . So I took a deep breath, crossed the room, and put the box on the table.

And do you know what?

Then my arms really started to ache. They felt strangely empty. It was like a burden *not* to be carrying that box. This feeling of supreme sadness flooded over me. It was all I could do to keep from crying.

"So am I done now?" I asked. "Are you going to send me home?"

Nimue stirred the fire. "Not yet. I believe Morgan le Fey will join us here."

I don't know how much time went by. Five minutes, ten minutes. Maybe even an hour. But that feeling of sadness just kept getting stronger. There was this big lump in my throat and silent tears were streaming down my face. I couldn't say anything, couldn't move, couldn't *think*. And looking back on it now, I believe Nimue must have been feeling pretty much the same way. Because she let the fire die, and the room grew cold.

Too cold.

I shivered. And that's when I *knew*. Someone was coming.

I tried to cry out, to warn Nimue. But my voice didn't work anymore. Neither did my arms or legs—like in one of those paralyzing nightmares that leaves you helpless, even after you're awake. So I just watched as the Time Shimmers formed a doorway, and Mordred stepped through.

Chapter 22

In My Two Hands

Right so there came by the holy vessel of the
Sangrail . . . and of that maiden that bare it, for
she was a perfect clean maiden. . . .
—Sir Thomas Malory,
Le Morte D'Arthur

Something flashed silver in Mordred's hand—a dagger maybe or that treacherous letter opener I'd seen at MBW. He grabbed Nimue's shoulders, pulled her back toward him, and held the blade to her throat.

"Bring me the box," he ordered, nodding toward the table.

But I still couldn't move.

"I said, bring me the box, girl." He tightened his grip on Nimue. Her eyes were closed, her mind quiet. What should I do?

Do as you're told.

Well, that did it. I mean, would you want Mordred's thoughts in *your* head? So without thinking, I grabbed the Grail box and rushed toward him like a football player. He released Nimue. She crumpled to the floor, limp as a pile of laundry. Then, as he started to step over her, Nimue uncurled like a cat, throwing Mordred off balance.

Run! her mind screamed into mine.

So I slipped through the door before the last of Mordred's Time Shimmers had sparkled into nothingness.

I flew down those stairs. Sure, the passageway was still dark and the steps were as steep as ever. But my necklace was glowing with a golden light far brighter than Nimue's lantern, so I saw everything clearly and knew exactly where to place my feet. Silently I thanked Morgan le Fey, wherever she was, for her gift.

That's when I heard Mordred, stumbling behind me, cursing in the dark. "You can't escape!" he shouted. "I have too many friends here!"

But I had my necklace, and for now that was all I needed. Still, when I reached the bottom of those stairs, I found myself wishing for a few friends of my own. Where should I go? What should I do next? If I went back to that courtyard, Sir Cai's people might be hanging around—or even Mordred's. They could mob me there. Then I heard his footsteps on the stairs. They were closer now, faster. So I turned and charged up that passageway under the second stone arch, where we'd seen that couple looking for the cat.

My necklace glowed as bright as a dozen flashlights. It showed me everything: the glistening stone walls, the smooth floor, every twist and turn in that cold, narrow passage. I ran and ran and ran until my socks got so wet from all the damp that they'd slipped under my heels. I kicked them off and kept going. And the Grail box? My arms must have found some kind of superhuman strength, my legs too. Because I wasn't working up a sweat or anything.

When I thought I'd gone far enough, I stopped and listened for Mordred. But if he was following me, he was as silent as a snake, which gave me the creeps. I mean, was he right behind me, relying on some kind of magic of his own? Maybe he could cast a spell and turn invisible—or maybe his Pendragon ring was as magical as my necklace. I started running again.

The passageway twisted and turned and curved in on itself. It spiraled in and out, around and around for what seemed like forever, always cold, damp, narrow. Finally, I rounded one last corner and found myself in some kind of entryway. Rows of torches burned bright. A thick carpet of purple, gold, and red tapestry led up to a short stairway. Beyond that? A door.

I raced up the steps and pushed against it. At first, the door didn't budge. Then I pushed again, remembering to concentrate, remembering to use the magic in my necklace. Finally, slowly, the door *creaked* open—so loud that if Mordred was anywhere within at least one hundred miles, he would know *exactly* where I'd gone.

Once inside, I leaned against the back of the door to get my bearings. Golden candleholders shaped like Grail creatures hung all along the hall. Between the candleholders, the walls were covered floor to ceiling, with tapestries—beautiful, intricate tapestries. Slowly, I walked down that hall, clutching the Grail box close. It was like being in an art museum, where the tapestries were works of art, like landscapes or portraits or scenes from a story: a boy pulling a sword from an anvil on a stone; a girl with long blond hair, twined through and through with wildflowers; a woman's arm reaching out of a lake and brandishing another sword. So then I knew. These were stories I'd heard from Mom, King Arthur's stories. . . .

At the end of the hall, I could see the nighttime sky—and a balcony. Moonlight spilled across its smooth, polished stone. The sound of voices, people talking fast, floated up from the ground below. So I crept closer, until I could hear every word.

"I avow the maid is a paltry thing," a man was saying. "But by all that is a wonderment, she carries the Grail, a marvelous treasure which we are bound to take by force."

Well, maybe I should just translate from here on out.

What he meant was that I wasn't important—and the Grail was. And *that* meant that Mordred had been telling the truth: His people *were* looking for me.

Another voice said something like, "He pays well. He always does."

I had to get a look at those two. So before I knew it, I was standing in the doorway of the balcony and there he was.

The king!

King Arthur himself. Who else could it have been? The crown, the sword, the purple cape, and . . . a Pendragon ring, exactly like Mordred's. The king was all by himself, leaning against the railing, listening (like me) to the conversation in the courtyard below. He turned and looked right at me.

Never in all my life have I seen eyes so sad and kind and lonely. He put a finger to his lips, and we just stood there until the men below moved away.

But by then, the conversation that had drawn me to that balcony didn't matter anymore. Neither did anything else. Not the Grail, not Mordred, not even his raven-haired kid. Because there was something absolutely magnetic about the king. The way he looked at you, you wanted to do the right thing, no matter what it took.

"Your Highness," I whispered.

I was just starting to do this little curtsy that I'd remembered from kindergarten, when he lightly touched my elbow and pulled me up.

"Grail Keeper," he whispered back.

But we'd run out of time.

"How touching," a voice sneered. Mordred's voice.

He stripped the Grail box from me and cradled it in one arm. Then he yanked me against his body, cold metal at my neck, the prickle of a knife against my skin.

"Stay where you are, Uncle, or the girl dies," Mordred ordered.

"Save the Grail, your Highness," I found myself saying. "I won't have a life worth saving if he keeps it."

But it was like the king hadn't heard me.

"You cannot change the course of history," the king said, moving toward us. His voice was deep and strong. "What is to be will be. The maid has played her part; let her go."

"Fool!" Mordred stepped back, dragging me with him. "Merlin knew nothing of destiny. I have defeated you and I have defeated Time. Behold!"

Then he released me. Just like that—and started fumbling with the Grail box. But suddenly, clearly, I felt his thoughts, Mordred's thoughts. Reaching, searching, calling up the words of that charm. I had to stop those words. Somehow, some way.

"The king is right, you know. Merlin was the Time master, not you."

Mordred glared up at me. He pried open the box with his dagger. So I tried again.

"Your magic is pathetic," I cried. "You lack the clarity of vision to possess the Grail, to master it, to touch it."

King Arthur met my gaze. "The maid speaks the truth," he said, turning to Mordred. "Your magic is wanton and dark. You have not the power."

Mordred's eyes glittered wild and crazy. "Grail Keeper blood courses through my veins. I can master the Grail more masterfully than your little maid." He laughed. "I will show you, Father."

The way he said *father* sounded obscene, like it was the most disgusting insult you could possibly imagine in any language. Then Mordred reached into the box, flung away the velvet wrappings. A burst of Time Shimmers cut through the air. Again, he reached into the box, still laughing, laughing, laughing.

Until he touched the Grail.

A blinding amber light shot out over the whole balcony. Mordred screamed. The Grail slipped from his hands and clattered to the floor. His body crumpled, his hands stripped of skin where he'd touched the Grail. Blood gushed from the corners of his eyes—his sightless eyes— just like Amanda Blessing. What kind of power was this? What kind of dark magic?

Even the king had turned away. The light was too much for him.

But I could see! I saw *right through* the Grail light, and as it grew stronger, my fears grew weaker. Because I knew. I *Saw*. Pure energy, pure light. That source of magic and power that inspires art and music and story, everything that nourishes the human spirit, everything that makes us dream. Beyond ourselves. Beyond Time. Then I heard a chorus of voices, the voices of the Grail goddess and her creatures.

Now, Grail Keeper. Now!

So I knelt by the Grail and picked it up in my two hands. My hands! Now the voices were singing—a joyous, wordless, soundless song that only I could hear. And the Grail sent out this feeling of—I don't know—well-being, happiness, contentment. The feeling shot through my arms, then up into my head, then down through my heart and into my legs. This wonderful, happy feeling of pure joy.

I walked past the king; past Mordred, still hunched on the floor; past his men, lying stunned in the hall; past the queen's servants gathered around the doorway. I just kept walking toward this cluster of amber and purple lights, the Shimmers of Time straight ahead, directly ahead—where Morgan le Fey and Nimue were waiting with outstretched arms. I stepped inside that circle of dancing light and passed the Grail to Morgan le Fey.

"You have done well, Grail Keeper," she said in a solemn voice. "Now the future lies ahead, unblemished and whole, as it was meant to be."

Then a doorway of Time Shimmers opened, and we passed out of that circle of light into a misty darkness.

The Time Shimmers faded into drifting petals—apple blossoms from the orchards of Avalon.

"Is it over now?" I asked.

Morgan le Fey said nothing. And for the first time, I noticed the dark bruise on her cheek, her bare shoulder showing through a slash in her clothes.

"Are you okay? What happened back there—in my Time?"

It is unimportant now.

And that was the last thought Morgan le Fey ever sent me. But she ran her hand against my cheek, very softly, before turning away.

"The Grail is safe," Nimue whispered, "and that's all that matters. Come," she said, leading me toward the lake. "You must return to your own Time and live the life you were destined to live."

We stopped at the water's edge. I looked back where we'd left Morgan le Fey. She was gone, as if she'd never existed—except in my imagination. So I had to ask, "Will I remember any of this?"

Nimue smiled and kissed me on the forehead. Then, without even saying good-bye, she raised her arms and summoned the Time Shimmers. I saw her for maybe half a second, then there was nothing but sparkles and the wind—the winds of Time.

The clouds came and went. The shimmers flickered out, and I was alone again in that dark, dark tunnel. Maybe, just maybe I saw Raven Head, a ghostly-looking shape chasing after shadows. But who can say? My mind might have been playing tricks on me. Because as soon as I thought I saw him, he was gone. And in his place were the Grail creatures, crowding all around me—sending me back through Time like old familiar friends.

Epilogue

Here is the end of the whole book. . . . I pray you all, gentlemen and gentlewomen that readeth this book . . . from the beginning to the ending, pray for me that God send me good deliverance. . . .
—Sir Thomas Malory,
Le Morte D'Arthur

Usually when you get to the end of a story like this, the main character wakes up and it was all a dream. Or her memories have been sucked out like the insides of an Easter egg, so she just mindlessly gets back to normal. Well, that's not exactly what happened to me. In fact, I proved Dad wrong. He always says nobody gets a second chance. Well, I did.

Kind of.

But first, I have to confess. I did wake up the very next morning back in bed at Maiden's Cottage. Only I remembered everything. So when Mom came in to tell me the big news, I thought I knew what she was going to say. You know, "They've found something really important on Glastonbury Tor—maybe the Holy Grail or something." Because obviously, we were reliving the past.

But that's *not* what Mom said.

"I've been invited to work with Dr. Ian Frazer," she announced.

Invited! Well, that was a surprise. But I should have known things were changing, even then. I mean, Dr. Frazer hadn't even been to tea with us yet!

Anyway, Mom babbled on, you know the way she does when she gets excited. Something about a precious, rare manuscript just discovered in a secret passageway below the ruins on Glastonbury Tor. "Dr. Frazer believes I may hold the key to its translation."

And she did. Maybe it's the Grail Keeper in her. Who knows? Anyway, the whole manuscript was about the Lady of the Lake, Nimue, Merlin, and the Grail. Mom thinks it pretty much proves that King Arthur was as real as you or me. In fact, she and Dr. Frazer just finished a couple of books about all this stuff not too long ago.

And Dr. Gildas? Well, the manuscript gave his museum a new lease on life, but it kind of undid his career. Remember? Dr. Gildas was the one who'd insisted King Arthur was a fairy tale—not real history or anything.

And what about me?

Turns out, I had a fairly interesting summer in Glastonbury. For example, Mom actually let Dr. Frazer give me some driving lessons. He taught me how to parallel park. Perfectly. I mean, if I can parallel park an old Landcruiser while sitting in a driver's seat on the right and shifting on the left, I can do almost anything. So I'm 90 percent sure I'll get my license before Erin.

Then I landed an internship with the Chalice Trust in Glastonbury, where I started my own kind of research into ESP and how it sometimes runs in families. Mom and I got pretty good at it. So good that one afternoon while Mom and I were flashing thoughts back and forth, we told Dr. Frazer *exactly* where he should dig: He found one of those clay vials like Morgan le Fey used to carry around all the time.

Still, I had to be pretty careful. Like when I said something about Merlin Nimuet's library and Mom looked at me like I'd lost my mind, because she'd never heard of anybody named Merlin Nimuet in her whole life, much less his library. But when we were at the airport, getting ready to go home, I had to check just one more thing. I looked up advertising agencies in the phone book, and you guessed it—there wasn't a listing for MBW. Or Vivian Nimuet. Or Crystal DuLac.

So by now, you're probably thinking, "I bet Felicity Jones just made this whole thing up." But I swear it's all true—and I have proof. My amber necklace.

I'm wearing it now. See?

Author's Note

In 1976, I enrolled in a graduate seminar on the Arthurian legend at the University of South Dakota. Although I found the subject fascinating, I was at a loss when I had to choose a research topic; Professor Thomas Gasque came to my rescue. "Look into the Grail legend and Glastonbury Tor," he suggested. What emerged was a report entitled "Joseph of Arimathea and Avalon"—and a lifelong passion for anything Arthurian.

I went on to write a master's thesis on novelist Doris Lessing, but Avalon had captured my heart. Over the next ten years, I read and reread Arthurian fiction and nonfiction, poetry and romance. Finally, in 1986, I started work on my first young adult novel—*The Last Grail Keeper,* a story about a reluctant young seer named Felicity Jones and the sinister Geoffrey Mordreaut. I finished a preliminary draft in 1993, but on the advice of a very wise editor, I filed it away and started writing something else. Felicity's story wasn't ready yet. It needed more time in the cauldron.

But her story stayed with me, and so did the idea of Grail Keepers, a long line of women trained in ancient mysteries, the tantalizing magic that shimmers just below the surface of virtually all Arthurian stories—from the Lady of the Lake, who gives young Arthur his sword, to the three queens, who bear the dying king to the Isle of Avalon.

The idea of Grail maidens came straight out of Sir Thomas Malory, who gives his readers glimpses of beautiful young women who understand the Grail's mysteries when Arthur's knights do not. I also adapted ideas from author Joseph Campbell. He maintained that the archetype behind the Holy Grail was probably Celtic—and perhaps even pre-Celtic. These two fragmentary ideas became the foundation for *The Last Grail Keeper.*

If indeed the Grail was Celtic, then it would have been a cauldron, not an elegant, shapely cup. In Welsh and Irish mythology, cauldrons are often the source of creativity, inspiration, healing, or even life itself. Archaeologists have uncovered cauldrons in Celtic sites all across Europe. In fact, the Gundestrup Cauldron, unearthed in Denmark during the 1890s, served as my inspiration for Felicity's Grail.

The Grail's association with the Lady of the Lake isn't entirely my own idea. Celtic cauldrons appear to have a close connection to water, which the ancient Celts viewed as a sacred life force. Many cauldrons have been uncovered near lakes, marshes, or streams and may have been women's ritual offerings.

I'm indebted to many writers for their originality and clarity of vision—from Sir Thomas Malory to Marion Zimmer Bradley, from Geoffrey Ashe (who graciously met with me in Glastonbury to answer my questions) to T. H. White. Especially T. H. White. Perhaps the bibliography that follows will spark your own quest to know more about the Grail and the Arthurian stories that inspired it.

Bibliography

Abrams, M. H., ed., *The Norton Anthology of English Literature Revised.* Vol. 1. New York: W. W. Norton & Company, Inc., 1968.

Ashe, Geoffrey. *Avalonian Quest.* London: Fontana Paperbacks, 1984.

———. *Mythology of the British Isles.* London: Methuen London, 1992.

———. Personal interview. 12 September 1999.

———. *The Discovery of King Arthur.* New York: Henry Holt and Company, 1985.

———. *The Landscape of King Arthur.* New York: Henry Holt and Company, 1987.

———. *The Traveller's Guide to Arthurian Britain.* Glastonbury, England: Gothic Image Publications, 1997.

Bendinger, Bruce. *The Copy Workshop Workbook.* Chicago: The Copy Workshop, 1993.

Bradley, Marion Zimmer. *The Mists of Avalon.* New York: Alfred A. Knopf, Inc., 1982.

225

Brengle, Richard, ed. *Arthur, King of Britain: History, Romance, Chronicle & Criticism.* New York: Appleton-Century-Crofts , 1964.

Campbell, Joseph. *The Masks of the Gods: Creative Mythology.* Penguin Books, 1976.

Cavendish, Richard. *King Arthur & The Grail: The Arthurian Legends and Their Meaning.* New York: Taplinger Publishing Company, 1979.

Christian, Catherine. *The Pendragon.* New York: Alfred A. Knopf, Inc., 1978.

Cunliffe, Barry. *The Ancient Celts.* New York: Oxford University Press, 1997.

Ellis, Peter Berresford. *The Ancient World of the Celts.* New York: Barnes and Noble Books, 1998.

———. *The Druids.* Grand Rapids, Mich.: William B. Eerdmans Publishing Company, 1995.

Fortune, Dion. *Glastonbury: Avalon of the Heart.* York Beach, Maine: Samuel Weiser, Inc., 2000.

Goodrich, Norma Lorre. *The Holy Grail.* New York: HarperCollins, 1992.

Green, Miranda J. *The World of the Druids.* London: Thames and Hudson, 1997.

Howard-Gordon, Frances. *Glastonbury: Maker of Myths.* Glastonbury, England: Gothic Image Publications, 1997.

Lacy, Norris J., ed. *The Arthurian Encyclopedia.* New York: Peter Bedrick Books, 1986.

Loomis, Roger Sherman. *The Development of Arthurian Romance*. New York: W. W. Norton & Company, Inc. 1970.

Malory, Sir Thomas. *Le Morte d'Arthur*. Vol. 1. New York: Penguin Books, 1986.

———. *Le Morte d'Arthur*. Vol. 2. New York: Penguin Books, 1976.

Markale, Jean. *Women of the Celts*. Rochester, Vt.: Inner Traditions International, Ltd., 1975.

Stewart, Mary. *The Crystal Cave*. New York: William Morrow and Company, Inc., 1970.

———. *The Last Enchantment*. New York: William Morrow and Company, Inc., 1979.

———. *The Wicked Day*. New York: William Morrow and Company, Inc., 1983.

Sutcliff, Rosemary. *The Road to Camlann*. New York: Puffin Books, 1981.

———. *The Sword and the Circle*. New York: Puffin Books, 1981.

White, T. H. *The Once and Future King*. New York: Berkley Medallion Books, 1966.

Woolley, Persia. *Child of the Northern Spring*. New York: Poseidon Press, 1987.

———. *Guinevere: The Legend in Autumn*. New York: Poseidon Press, 1991.

———. *Queen of the Summer Stars*. New York: Poseidon Press, 1990.